Five to Five

D. ERSKINE MUIR

With an introduction by Curtis Evans

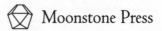 Moonstone Press

This edition published in 2021 by Moonstone Press
www.moonstonepress.co.uk

Introduction © 2021 Curtis Evans

Originally published in 1934 by Methuen & Co. Ltd, London

Five to Five © 1934 The Estate of D. Erskine Muir

The right of Dorothy Erskine Muir to be identified as author of this work has
been asserted in accordance with the Copyright, Designs and Patents Act 1988

ISBN 978-1-899000-42-5
eISBN 978-1-899000-43-2

A CIP catalogue record for this book is available from the British Library

Text designed and typeset by Tetragon, London
Cover illustration by Jason Anscomb
Printed and bound by CPI Group (UK) Ltd, Croydon, CRO 4YY

Contents

Introduction by Curtis Evans   7

CHARACTERS   13

I   The Watcher   15
II   The Prey   21
III   The Tea-Party   33
IV   The Return   49
V   The Dead   61
VI   The Detective   75
VII   The Dealer   85
VIII   The Heir   99
IX   The Hypothesis   113
X   The Suspects   123
XI   The Doctor   139
XII   The Wife   151
XIII   The Artist   163
XIV   The End   175
XV   The First Solution   185
XVI   The Complete Case   197

Introduction

At seven o'clock on the evening of Monday, 21 December, an old lady, living alone with one servant in a comfortable flat in a well-to-do Glasgow street, was brutally butchered on her dining-room hearthrug, during the temporary absence of the maid to buy an evening paper. The victim was Miss Marion Gilchrist, eighty-three years of age, a person of reserved and solitary habits, only remarkable in that she possessed some £3,000 of jewels, which she kept hidden among her dresses in her wardrobe.

—"The Slater Case", in *Knave's Looking Glass* (1935) by William Roughead

The murder in Glasgow of octogenarian jewel-fancier Miss Marion Gilchrist remains unsolved today, likely largely because the original investigation by Scottish police into the crime and its circumstances was either astonishingly inept or criminally complicit in the dread deed. The great Scottish criminologist William Roughead—he will be familiar to those of you who have already read Dorothy Erskine Muir's first true-crime-inspired detective novel, *In Muffled Night* (1933), which draws on another of Glasgow's notorious unsolved murders, the 1862 Jessie McLachlan case—was associated with the Gilchrist murder case for years, having:

(1) attended the original trial of Oscar Slater, the man accused of the crime, in 1909;

(2) authored *Trial of Oscar Slater* for the Notable British Trials Series, which highlighted the gaping flaws in the state's case, in 1910;

(3) published a revised edition of the book, with even more damning detail, in 1925;

(4) served as a witness at the hearing of Oscar Slater's successful appeal against his now nineteen-year-old prison sentence in 1928;

(5) published a final revised edition of *Oscar Slater* in 1929;

(6) produced a concise account of "The Slater Case" in his collection of criminological essays *Knave's Looking Glass*, in 1935.

"The Slater Case" was reprinted in 1951, a year before Roughead's death at the age of eighty-two, in his penultimate book, *Classic Crimes*, a brilliantly cut jewel of true-crime writing that was reprinted in 2000 by New York Review Books in a fine edition that happily remains in print and available throughout the world today. The essay makes compelling if infuriating reading, as Roughead methodically demolishes the state's absurd case against the man whom it successfully prosecuted for Marion Gilchrist's bloody murder.

The police errors (?) in the Slater case were both manifold and grievous. As Roughead notes, with a fortune in jewels (worth some £315,000/$450,000 today) at her elbow, "Miss Gilchrist was morbidly afraid of robbers," and had made unsanctioned ingress into her domain a daunting procedure indeed; so it seems highly unlikely that the murderer—who had managed to gain entrance to the flat, presumably, during the perilously brief absence of the live-in maid, Helen Lambie—would have been unknown to the victim. When Lambie returned and entered her mistress's flat in the company of a neighbour, Arthur Adams, who resided downstairs with his two sisters (a few minutes earlier all three of them had heard loud noises emanating from the flat above), they encountered a gentleman, purportedly unrecognized by them, departing the premises. Yet another witness—a fourteen-year-old message girl named Mary Barrowman, who claimed to be in the street at the time (although this claim was challenged)—stated as well that she saw a man running down the steps of the building. Although the police inferred from the disparate descriptions given by the three eyewitnesses that the man leaving the flat and the man running down the stairs were not actually one and the same person, they later altered this view, after they had alighted on a suspect, a thirty-six-year-old native German Jew of rather dubious background named Oscar Slater, upon whom they proceeded crudely to pin the crime.

According to Helen Lambie, out of the hoard of jewellery in her mistress's flat only a diamond brooch was actually missing. (Miss Gilchrist's papers had been disturbed as well.) When the police discovered that Oscar Slater had recently pawned a diamond brooch before departing for the United States (a trip planned before the murder took place), this set them on his trail. Even after it was learned that Slater's brooch was actually a different article from Miss Gilchrist's missing one (thus rendering the "brooch clue" entirely worthless) and the police failed to establish that their suspect even knew the victim, they clung tenaciously, like a pug on a trouser leg, to the belief that Slater was their man. After a farcical identity parade and constant honing of the eyewitnesses' recollections, he was brought to trial, convicted on a 9–6 verdict (this being Scotland, unanimity was not required) and sentenced to death by a piously overbearing judge who set a new standard in prejudicial judicial sanctimony.

It is no wonder that the Slater case, like the McLachlan case before it, provoked outrage and protest among thousands of individuals, including, famously, Edinburgh native Sir Arthur Conan Doyle, creator of Sherlock Holmes, who damned the entire official proceeding as a "lamentable story of official blundering from start to finish". As in the case of Jessie McLachlan nearly half a century earlier, Oscar

Slater's death sentence was commuted to a term of life imprisonment, of which, as mentioned above, he served nineteen years. All in all, it was surely one of the clearest cases of judicial injustice in Scottish legal history.

For many decades accounts of the Slater case were less concerned with the question of *whodunit* than with *what in hell was done to him?* In other words, writers about the affair mostly devoted themselves to pointing out the manifold structural weaknesses in the shaky scaffolding which the state had erected in support of Slater's shameful conviction. However, in *Five to Five*, D. Erskine Muir's second detective novel, the author went looking for another killer. In her review of the novel in the *Sunday Times*, Dorothy L. Sayers noted that the Gilchrist enigma was one of the most "mysterious of all recent murder cases", with the quashing of Slater's sentence having been unsatisfactorily "based on technical grounds which shed no further light upon the central problem of who really did the murder". "Mr. [*sic*] Muir" had, Sayers added, "used the opening situation [in the Slater case] as the thesis for an exciting and well-constructed murder story... with a dramatic and soundly argued conclusion".

Admittedly lacking in the story is the real-life high drama of a monstrously stigmatized man unjustly tried and convicted for a crime he did not commit, but in its place readers will find an engaging murder problem constructed with all the sober rigour of Freeman Wills Crofts and enriched with Muir's superior descriptive power and skill at the drawing of character. Additionally, we also are treated to a return engagement, after his winning appearance in *In Muffled Night*, with the upright and tenacious Detective Inspector Woods of the CID, with whom Crofts' own Inspector French doubtlessly would have been honoured to serve. Readers who peruse further in the stacks of Slateriana that have accumulated over the decades—Roughead's "The Slater Case" certainly would be a good place to start—will find additional instances, like those concerning the murder weapon and the mysterious "watcher" from across the way, where Muir has drawn on the real-life-crime problem in constructing her fictional one. Surely to the mystery of the cruel slaying of Mr. Simon Ewing, that disagreeable, elderly and infirm collector of jade and jewels, the author has come up with a far more credible solution than the Scottish authorities ever managed to do during their infamous investigation into the murder of Miss Marion Gilchrist.

CURTIS EVANS
Germantown, TN
28 June 2021

CHARACTERS

SIMON EWING

PENELOPE FORDHAM

HENRY GODFREY

ANNE GODFREY

DOREEN GODFREY

MRS. DUTTON

NURSE EDWARDS

MR. HETHERINGTON

DETECTIVE-INSPECTOR WOODS

DETECTIVE-SERGEANT RILEY

GEORGE FORDHAM

DR. AINSLIE

NOTE

All the above characters are fictitious and have no reference to any living person or persons.

Chapter I

THE WATCHER

There was the warmth and light—
The sense of life so just an inch inside—

Half-Rome, R. BROWNING.

The rain slanted down, quietly and steadily. It was cold, and the man standing in the street shifted uneasily from one foot to the other. He had been standing there for some little time, his back pressed against the railings of the area of the empty house. Now he moved slowly along the dripping pavement, glancing up and down as he slouched along, collar turned up, hands in pockets.

The rain-soaked street was silent and deserted. Only a subdued roar of traffic from the great main road, some little distance away, echoed through the air. No traffic passed along this quiet backwater. Situated in Kensington, not far from the chief shopping area, it was yet extraordinarily isolated. The houses were of the familiar London brick, once pale yellow, now dark. Originally built as large family houses, they were now mostly split up into flats or maisonettes. The road was a short one, curving away from the spot where the watcher stood. He had been loitering between two houses, one empty, the other with a brass plate which bore the name "Dr. Ainslie". Opposite to him a street lamp shone across the wet road. Its light fell upon the entrances to the flats behind it, forming part of a block of converted houses. Actually the three or four at that end of the street belonged to the "Residential Hotel" at the corner. The proprietress there, who had made a success of her business, had bought up the adjoining houses and turned them into good flats, which were served from her hotel, and had a passage built on at the back communicating with her restaurant.

The man in the raincoat turned at the sound of a motor coming round the corner behind him. It was Dr. Ainslie's car, and, as if anxious to avoid being seen, the watcher went hurriedly up the steps of an entrance beyond and vanished under the portico. This belonged to a set of self-contained flats, and in consequence the main door into the hall was open. Standing within and glancing back, the man saw that the doctor, instead of stopping in front of his own house, was drawing up at the one where he himself was sheltering, and was evidently intending to pay a visit within.

After a moment's hesitation, the man, clearly wishing to avoid a meeting with the doctor, began to ascend the staircase. He paused on the first landing, but hearing the doctor's quick footsteps beginning to mount behind him, went on up the next flight. The doctor halted on the first floor; a pause, and then came the faint sound of a bell trilling in one of the flats. The man above stood still, listening and waiting. From his position now it chanced that he could see out of the window, which, facing towards the street, lit up the staircase at the turn. He stared out. Across the dusk a light shone brightly. It came from one of the flats on the opposite side of the road. A room on the first floor had been left with blinds undrawn. The interior showed as a lit-up stage shines across the dark auditorium. From the street level no view into this room had been possible, but from his present position the watcher could look down and across and see everything within. Stepping to the window, he leant his arms on the sill and gazed eagerly out.

Three long windows faced him. They gave a clear view into a very beautiful room, contrasting rather sharply with the drab exterior of the buildings. Tall glass-fronted cabinets were ranged against soft green walls; a few large pieces of oriental china were placed here and there. A great copper bowl filled with pink and white lilies took up the whole of a table near the windows. Mirrors in lacquer frames gleamed on the few spaces left on the walls between the cabinets, and a big lacquer screen apparently stood before the door. On the hearth a fire of sea-logs sent off those bright blue flames which are advertised as a special attraction by firms of ship-breakers. The light sparkled into the room and was reflected back by the shining objects with which the cabinets were filled.

In a big arm-chair with an invalid's foot-extension, drawn up close to the hearth, sat a man. He had white hair and, as far as could be seen, a pale, thin, waxen face. He had a special sort of baize-covered board in front of him, resting on the arms of the chair. This was evidently used as a writing-table, for some sheets of paper were scattered on it, and he held something in his hand which appeared to be a pen, for as the watcher looked on he began to write. A tall standard lamp in a beautiful oriental design was placed close to the arm-chair. The light, falling softly downwards, showed quite clearly the glint of his white head bending forward over his papers. The fireplace was in the middle of the wall to the left of the watcher. Between it and the window stood a bureau, with a tall open top, consisting of two doors, folded back now and showing an elaborate arrangement of small drawers and pigeonholes. On the rug before the hearth knelt a girl, whose fair hair caught the gleam of the flickering flames. She was busily picking up something from the floor. Her hands moved backwards and forwards, seeming to tidy with swift movements. Presently she rose, and pressed whatever she had collected in her hands down into a waste-paper basket standing by the corner of the hearth. She walked across the room and disappeared behind the screen. Presently she reappeared, now wearing a waterproof, and pausing in front of one of the mirrors began to adjust her beret. The elderly man laid down his pen and turned towards her. From the depths of his arm-chair he fished up some small packet which he held out towards the girl. She took it, but with a curious stiff little gesture, and with a perceptible pause of hesitation. The man then pulled from his breast-pocket a wallet and handed the girl what was clearly money in the shape of bank-notes. The girl put this and the little packet into her hand-bag, and then, turning away, began to pick up a number of parcels from a chair which was out of the range of sight from the window. Both girl and man glanced towards the mantelpiece. Following an imperious gesture from the old man, the girl, awkwardly balancing the pile of parcels on one arm, stepped towards the tall windows, and with her free hand began to pull the cords which worked the curtains. Slowly as she tugged, the heavy folds began to slip across the lighted spaces. She went from one window to the other, until finally, again with that faint reminiscence of the theatre, the last fold swung into place, and the bright interior was shut away.

The watcher opposite still did not stir, but stood motionless and intent. Presently the front door across the street opened. The girl came out and stood to open her umbrella beneath the big portico. Then, running down the steps, she turned to her right and went swiftly down the street.

At this very moment the watcher was startled by a sudden outburst of voices coming from below.

"Very well, I'll run up, doctor, and see if Miss Stack would let me use her telephone," and hasty steps could be heard mounting the stone staircase towards the landing. Instantly the man turned, and began with great speed to go up still higher. On the floor above two doors faced him, one on either hand, giving access to the small two-roomed apartments at this, the top of the house. The farther one had a card pinned on it: "Mr. Hetherington", Hastily crossing to it and keeping his back towards the person coming up behind him, the man pressed the bell, and while the woman was knocking and ringing with agitation at the nearer door he found himself confronted by a tall, burly figure wearing an artist's overall.

"Mr. Finlay?" he inquired in a rather low, husky voice.

"Certainly not," retorted the artist. "Can't you read?" pointing to the card fixed to the centre of the door by a drawing-pin.

"Sorry, I was told Mr. Finlay lived here," mumbled the watcher.

"Well, he doesn't; and the man who was here before wasn't called Finlay either. I've only moved in a couple of weeks, but the fellow before me was MacNaughton. You've come to the wrong block," and with these words, snapped over his shoulder, the peppery occupier of Flat 5 bounced back into his passage-hall, slamming the door in the inquirer's face.

By now, however, the agitated lady had been admitted to the opposite flat and the coast was clear. The watcher began to make his way down the staircase. He had hardly passed the lower landing, when he heard the door of the flat open, and the doctor's voice was audible, in the preliminaries of departure.

"Well, I must be off now, I'm afraid. I've an urgent case waiting. But the nurse will do all that's needed, and I'll look in again on my way home to dinner."

Hastening ahead, the man in the raincoat reached the front door. Slipping out, he glanced cautiously round, and as he did so a big clock in some nearby tower began to boom out its deep chimes. It was five o'clock, and as the heavy notes died away trembling through the damp air the man ran very hurriedly down the staircase and vanished into the rain.

Chapter II

THE PREY

Who are these you have let descend my stair?

Guido, R. BROWNING.

Had the watcher been at his post of vantage on the staircase a little earlier, he might have been even more astonished at what could be seen in the lighted flat. Astonished, but not, perhaps, more deeply interested, for nothing could have exceeded the absorption with which he had contemplated the commonplace little scene. A half-hour earlier, and no one would have failed to be intrigued by what that interior revealed. At that time, however, the watcher was below in the street, where the row of lighted-up windows across could of course be seen, but their height from the ground prevented anyone in the street seeing what went on within.

The flat belonged to the elderly man. He was by name Simon Ewing, by station a comparatively wealthy widower, and by disposition something of a tyrant. This might have been deduced from a study of his face.

He was an unusual-looking man. His limbs, though shrunken now, had formerly been those of a massive, well-proportioned frame. His features were strongly marked and finely modelled. A thin, high, hooked nose cut sharply down from the narrow forehead. His eyes were a cold blue, faded now by old age, but still capable of giving off a frosty sparkle. His lids drooped in a noticeable manner, being as it were folded over the eyes and lifting themselves when he glanced up. The effect was not exactly sinister, but it did produce the same impression as that given by a snake, of a complete lack of warmth, a feeling of coldness, of something faintly scaly and reptilian. His thin-lipped mouth and sunken cheeks strengthened this impression. The deep lines which gave harshness, but not dignity, were carved chiefly by ill-temper. A harsh, hard man, with no sympathy, would have been the verdict produced by a study of his face.

Yet his surroundings proclaimed him to be a man of taste. The room was full of beauty. The soft green colouring of the painted walls, the ceiling tinted to tone, the heavy velvet curtains, again of green but in a deeper shade, the chairs and sofas upholstered in green and gold, were clearly planned to harmonize with the contents of the beautiful cabinets which were placed all round the walls. The cabinets were in themselves lovely things, made of black and gold lacquer, with glass doors divided up into panels by strips of thin gilded wood. Within them were ranged rows upon rows of jade and crystal figures and boxes, mostly of green, but here and there of pink or milky white. The effect of their sheen reflected on every side, and throwing back the glow of the lamps and the sparkle of the fire's flames, was wonderfully gay and pleasing. This was the room of a connoisseur and a collector, a man, too, who probably chose deliberately to spend his money on this rare beauty within his walls rather than on mere grandeur in his surroundings. For the actual street and locality would hardly have led one to expect such an interior.

The girl who was the other occupant of the room scarcely looked as if she were a component part of the scene. She was young, not more than twenty-four or five, very slim, very pale, very pretty, with hair of a bright, pale gold. She was rather tall, and had noticeably fine hands and feet, long and slender. She did not, however, share the look of luxury which seemed to radiate from her surroundings. Her pallor was due to fatigue; her expression was sad and troubled. Her clothes, though becoming enough, were rather shabby and cheap. Plenty of character showed in her face: her mouth, with its firm, well-cut lines, the straight, clear, wide look of her eyes, the contour of her chin, all showed strength and self-restraint. Here was a woman who was not finding life easy, but who evidently was standing up to her difficulties, who was making a fight, and who knew how to hold her own.

She was, however, despite appearances, related to the elderly man, as her words revealed.

"Well, Uncle Simon, do you think these are all your parcels? Five I've done up now—the last five on your list."

"Don't interrupt me, please. I must get this letter finished to go off with Mrs. Connell's book," in a sharp, peremptory tone.

The fair-haired girl pressed her lips together angrily, and glanced at the figure bending over his writing-board; then, sitting back on her heels, began to gaze pensively at the fire. For a few moments there was no sound but the crackling from the flames and the sound of a pen moving rapidly over paper. Then, having signed his name with great firmness, the man leant back and, contemplating the girl, began to speak, still in the same harsh, sharp tones.

"As Nurse is out, I will take the opportunity to get you to do something for me. Kindly go and fetch me a black tin dispatch-box, Penelope; I'll tell you where you will find it." He added a few brief directions, and the girl went out, returning shortly, bearing by its handles a black japanned box, about twenty inches long by twelve broad and fifteen deep. Motioning to her to set it down on a square, high stool which was placed beside him, he produced a key from his pocket, and, unlocking the box, began to lift out a number of leather cases of various sizes and shapes. A bright flicker seemed suddenly to leap up in the girl's eyes as she saw this action, but instantly she appeared to draw herself together, and it was with apparent calm detachment that she stood silently watching and listening to the man, who now began to speak again.

"One thing I wish to say to you before you go, Penelope," he said, uttering his words slowly but very distinctly. "I dare say you'll be disappointed, though, of course, you have no right to be so. I have decided to send Nora, as her Christmas present this year, the large solitaire diamond ring which belonged to your aunt." He paused, and his words seemed to fall into a pool of silence, for the girl to whom he was speaking neither answered nor moved. He went on, with a slightly emphasized harshness in his tones: "I know, of course, that you always specially admired that ring, and as George would, in the natural order of events, expect to inherit that part of my possessions which came from your aunt's side of the family, I dare say you've supposed that ring would come to you one day. But I've come to the conclusion that as Nora is marrying so well I should wish to give her a handsome present this year, and I think she would appreciate the ring now, and wear it to more advantage than you could."

He looked up as he spoke, as if to emphasize by the glance he cast at the girl the unsuitability of coupling this talk of diamonds with her rather poverty-stricken appearance. Responsive to the shade of meaning in his tone, the girl flushed as she glanced down at her cheap woollen frock, and at her hands, which showed by a certain roughness and redness their quite unmistakable familiarity with housework.

Still she answered nothing, and, with a rather angry look directed towards her silent figure, the man turned back and began now to open the various little cases he had tumbled on to the board before him. One after the other he opened, but lifted nothing out, and, putting them carelessly aside, left their contents to sparkle and blaze in the light shining down upon them, while he sought for the particular thing he wanted. Beautiful as the room was, with clear evidence of a high standard of comfort, even then the modest character of the house and street without gave a certain air of incongruity to the heap of precious stones. For the pile of jewellery was not only extensive in itself, it was also amazing in its quality. Bracelets, necklaces, brooches, pendants lay there in profusion. Someone, it was clear, had known and loved the beauty of precious stones, and had indulged that taste. Some of the pieces were old-fashioned—conspicuous amongst them a necklace of large emeralds set with diamonds and pearls—but all were fine, and the value was clearly very great.

Hardly glancing at them, the man continued his search until he came upon a small oblong case, which on being opened showed itself as a box specially adapted to contain rings. Within, in two rows, were ranged about twenty, the coloured ones along one side of the box, sapphire, emerald, ruby, opal, and on the other side diamond and pearl hoops, and one or two of the marquise and solitaire patterns, set with what were obviously very fine stones. Picking out one of these, the man spoke again.

"I don't, of course, wish to hurt your feelings, Penelope"—this rather perfunctorily, for it was clear that, whatever might be wished, the effect of these words was certainly wounding—"but I think you must recognize for yourself that there is a great difference between your position and Nora's. Nora can wear this ring with perfect suitability; you, as I think you'll admit, can scarcely do so."

At this the girl could keep silence no longer. Clasping her hands tightly together, and moistening lips which had suddenly gone dry, she spoke, at first slowly and trying to pick her words, then with increasing speed as her self-control appeared to lessen.

"Of course, Uncle Simon, I do realize how different Nora's life is from mine, and I know too you have a perfect right to do as you please with Aunt Ada's things. But—" She hesitated, and then, making up her mind to continue, she went on: "I don't know; perhaps I shouldn't say anything at all, but I must; I can't just say nothing.

I must tell you we've always hoped you'd keep Aunt Ada's family things for us."

Again she paused, but the man, setting his thin lips more closely than ever, made no reply. He fitted the ring into a little case he had picked out of the box, and began to pile the other pieces back again. When he had replaced them all and relocked the box, he said briefly:

"Stand this down here in the corner beside me, Penelope."

The girl lifted the box and placed it in the position he indicated, down in the corner between the waste-paper basket and the nearest cabinet.

"Give me some brown paper and string, and the sealing-wax," he bade next.

She handed him a sheet of thick brown paper which he began methodically to divide up, throwing the unneeded fragments piece by piece into the basket. The girl watched him at his task for a few moments, with a look, partly bitter, partly almost wild, on her face, until, as if rendered desperate by the sight of these methodical movements and by his obstinate silence, she at length broke out, and having once begun went on boldly: "After all, we can't help feeling that some of those things"—she indicated with a faint motion of her hand the box, now once more hiding the heap of shining jewels—"did come from George's family. They belonged to his grandmother, and he's the only person left now on that side—naturally he'd like to have things he remembers and knows from old days, and not have them go to people who have no connexion with them."

While his fingers dealt rather clumsily with the making of the parcel, the man had been giving half his attention to the girl's words. Now, however, he had finished, and he turned towards her, speaking slowly and distinctly as he gazed at her with penetration.

"I don't admit the force of those arguments, Penelope. Sentimental reasons don't weigh with me. If George wants to appeal to my family feelings he hasn't gone the right way to work at all. He might, as my wife's only relation, perhaps have hoped I should consider he had some sort of claim upon me, but, as you both know perfectly well, I've not had occasion to be specially pleased with him, and certainly of late I've not felt at all inclined to do anything for him whatever. Nor should I think it at all desirable to give you a present which George might utilize for his own advantage."

The flush on Penelope's cheeks deepened, and she broke in:

"That's not kind of you, Uncle Simon. George may have been troublesome to you, indeed of course I know he has, but you might make allowances. He's been so awfully unlucky, and so many things have been against him. You can't blame him if he's wanted you to help him a little and has perhaps pestered you about his schemes. I dare say," she hurried on, seeing the clouds darkening on her uncle's face, "that he hasn't been very sensible or tactful in these last few weeks over this partnership he wants to try, and I know he's vexed you by the way he's urged you to help him. But you're the only person who *could* do anything for us, and oh! Uncle Simon, you don't know, you can't know, how awful it is to have such a chance as this, and to know if it once goes it'll never come again, and yet not be able to take it! You don't know what our life is—or what it would mean to get this good start!"

Here she was brought to an abrupt stop, for the man held up his hand with an angry, decisive gesture.

"Please stop this, Penelope! I will not listen to you! I do *not* mean to discuss the question. I've told George plainly the matter is finished and done with. I do not intend to advance him the money. Indeed, I could not do so without inconveniencing myself, and George has given me no inducement to do that."

"But, Uncle Simon," pleaded the girl, clearly feeling that here was the last opportunity, "don't you feel that George is your only relation?

You've no one of your own, and he's the only one left of Aunt Ada's family. He didn't have much of a chance as a boy, but I do believe if he could go into this partnership now, and be more on his own, he'd steady down and do better, and turn over a new leaf. Of course we wouldn't ever want you to do anything to inconvenience yourself, or to do without anything you need, but we can't but know—everyone does—that you might perhaps help us without depriving yourself of anything." Her glance flew, as if involuntarily, to the cabinets around the room, with their many little figures of jade and crystal, representing clearly a collection of no small value, and she hurried on:

"I know you need your money for your collection, and of course I know it's all the world to you, but, Uncle—couldn't you"—her eyes fell on the box containing the jewellery, standing down in the corner beside them; she hesitated for the fraction of a second, and then dashed on with the courage of despair—"wouldn't you, if you've no free cash to let us have at the moment, perhaps—as a special thing—let us have some of that jewellery *now?* You have told us both, before this, that eventually George was to have his grandmother's things. They're only kept locked up and put away, and if we could have even one piece now, just to raise these few hundred pounds, it would give George his chance."

She came to a stop, checked by the look on her uncle's face, and this time the anger both in his face and voice stopped her flow of entreaty.

"Penelope, kindly understand, once and for all, I do not intend, and shall never agree, to sell anything, either of my own or of what belonged to your aunt, in my lifetime, nor shall I make it possible for George to do so. What he and you may choose to do in the future is another matter. I shall only consider the present. George must depend on himself, and I have no intention whatever of making his way for him. He is the only one of my wife's family left, and, of course, I admit he has a moral claim upon me, but kindly realize he is only my nephew by marriage, and, devoted as my wife was to him, I have never, as you are aware, shared that feeling."

Roused by anger, he seemed on the verge of saying still more, but seeing the girl shrink back slightly as if alarmed by the fierce undertone of his voice, he pulled himself up abruptly and, with a slight return to his more frigid manner, added:

"I have no fault to find with you, Penelope, and indeed I am often sorry for you, as I know you have a great struggle to get along, and I know you make the best of things. So don't let us speak of this further. Kindly don't answer me"—quickly, as Penelope opened her lips—"Please let us say no more, and"—turning back to the little parcels—"if you would wait a few moments I will ask you to take this with you."

Conscious, perhaps, of the strain he was putting on the girl's self-control and politeness in giving her this unpleasing commission, he added: "I should not ask you to do this, but as Nurse Edwards is not back, and I wish the parcel posted and registered to-night, I must get you to take it;" and he went on as if glad in spite of himself to break the awkward silence created by the girl's lack of acquiescence: "I really can't think what has happened to Nurse. It is most vexatious. I distinctly told her to be back within half an hour, and she has been gone much more than that."

Penelope seemed to welcome the chance of reestablishing normal conversation.

"Well, the shops are sure to be very crowded just now. I expect she took a long time to get served, and, as I happened to come in, it really doesn't matter, does it? I can take your parcels to the post office on the way home."

"Yes, of course the parcels can be got off, but that is not quite what I meant," replied Mr. Ewing, busily glancing over the little pile of letters before him to make sure all were correctly addressed and stamped. "What I am objecting to is Nurse's unpunctuality. I really was reluctant to let her go out at all to-day. I have not been well, and it would, to my mind, have been better if she had given up her 'time out' as she calls it. But she was so urgent, and insisted that her shopping was important and would not keep her out long, that I gave way. I wish now I had stood firm. She knows perfectly well I expect her to be out for half an hour only in the afternoon, and no more. Dr. Ainslie wishes her to have this 'breath of fresh air', as he calls it, every day, but I find it most inconvenient, and if the time isn't adhered to quite strictly I shall certainly veto the arrangement. She gets out every morning to the shops and on messages, and this extra outing isn't to my mind at all necessary. I expected her to be back not later than a quarter-past four. I like her to get my tea ordered, and superintend it coming up from the restaurant herself at that hour. They're apt not to have things as I like them, and she knows how intensely I dislike waiting for my meals."

"I think she was late in starting out," said Penelope in a dispirited tone. She was disheartened by the result of her efforts, and, having been tired out before ever she came to see her uncle, the tension and excitement of their encounter had now produced a reaction intensified by her failure.

"How do you know that?" inquired Simon, rather severely.

"As I came up the street I saw her going down the steps and setting off in the opposite direction. I called after her, to let her know I was coming, but she didn't hear me, and went hurrying off as fast as she could go. It was just after four then, you know."

"In that case it was a pity you didn't run after her and catch her up," said Ewing, with an air of displeasure. "You know how intensely I dislike opening my door. Actually I am better to-day, and able just to hobble across the room, but it is mere chance that I was able to do so. I certainly should not have made the distinctly painful effort had

I not recognized your knock, and wished for you to help me with this business of Nora's ring." Then, as if catching himself up in the return to the subject they had dropped, he added a trifle more benignly: "But in any case I need not keep you longer, Penelope. You will want to be getting home yourself. Perhaps you would just tidy up the paper and so on before you go. I dislike seeing any untidiness. If you will put things straight I will just finish this one card."

The girl did as she was requested, and began to collect the fragments littering the hearth.

As she straightened herself, the old man held out to her the little parcel into which he had put the ring, and as he did so his glance went once more to the clock, and he realized it was even later than he had thought.

"You must please hurry, Penelope. I specially wish these parcels to catch the 5.30 country post. The office is sure to be terribly crowded, and it's nearly five minutes to the hour now. Drop the smaller ones in the big special box, but be sure to register the one to Nora." He drew out his note-case, and handed the girl some money. Perhaps in his heart he repented of that added request, for when the girl had gone he sat for a moment with his gaze fixed on the fire, frowning slightly, and pulling reflectively at his lower lip with his thin fragile fingers, as if not altogether well satisfied with what he had done. The sound of her footsteps echoed up to him for a moment as she ran down the front steps beneath him, but their quick, light tapping on the pavement rapidly died away in the distance. A mental picture rose before him of her slim figure speeding away through the raw damp of the winter evening. He sat there in the warmth and glow, surrounded with the colour and the luxury he loved. Had he been able to go to the window, he would have seen the light of the street lamp strike for a moment on her golden hair as she hurried on through the drizzling rain. He might have seen, too, another figure which, at the same moment, emerged from the dark doorway opposite, and which, with hat pressed down low over the eyes, now came hastening towards him across the dripping road.

Chapter III

THE TEA-PARTY

Easy to say, easy to do, step right
Now you've stepped left.

Tertium Quid, R. BROWNING.

There is a fascination to be felt in walking homewards on a wet evening, seeing the gleam of light from windows, perhaps the flicker of firelight on a ceiling, and knowing that soon one will turn out of the damp and cold of the street into a warm, bright room.

Something of the sort was passing through the mind of Henry Godfrey as he turned up the steps and rang the bell of No. 5A Clevedon Street. Certainly the evening was raw and unpleasant, and he had every confidence in the warmth and comfort he would find within. He was coming to have tea, and pick up his wife, at the flat where his aunt, Mrs. Dutton, lived. Godfrey himself lived down in Putney, but to-night he had left his office early and had come round to Kensington. Glancing upwards as he waited to be admitted to the flat, he could see that Simon Ewing, in whose collection of jade he was interested, was at home, for the light shone through the chinks of the row of tall windows above. Reflecting that he might possibly find it opportune to go up before he and his wife went on home, he turned now as the door before him opened, and his sister Anne welcomed him in. She did not live there, but had come now to spend Christmas with her aunt.

Mrs. Dutton's maisonette had not the style and elegance of her neighbour, Mr. Ewing's. She had the lower part of the house, including the basement. She thus had two very large rooms on the ground-floor, formerly the dining-room and study behind, which, in her case, now were respectively her big living-room in front and her bedroom behind. Downstairs she had a room in front, which she had turned into her spare-room, looking, really, into the area. The steps leading down, however, had been taken away, and the windows were barred, so that there was no possible entrance to the room that way. The rest of the basement she used as box-room and a tiny kitchen, for like many other dwellers in service flats she preferred occasionally to provide herself with light meals which she cooked herself. As she had the original ground-floor and entrance, she should have had a large square entrance hall. When, however, the house was converted, half of the hall was divided off in order to provide a separate entrance to the flat above. She still was left, however, with a good broad passage-way, once the narrow entrance itself was passed, and this gave an air of spaciousness to the house.

The furniture was of the kind so often met with in the houses of good middle-class English families. A few beautiful chests and chairs and mirrors; some good Persian rugs, gay chintz, brass bowls filled with ferns, rather too many pictures on the walls, and too many pieces of china and knick-knacks on the tables; a dearth of books; a general air of comfort and of enjoyment in harmonious colours, and well-polished furniture. Nothing very original or striking, but everything agreeable and bright.

Entering the hall, Godfrey took off his wet raincoat, hung it up, banged his umbrella down into the stand with an air of relief, and followed his sister into the room on the left, which faced into the street and was actually the room beneath Simon Ewing's sitting-room in the flat above. In the Dutton's flat this big living-room was, at the moment, rather untidy in appearance, for scattered over it were numbers of parcels, sheets of paper, cardboard boxes, and all the impedimenta of parcels yet to be done up. Christmas preparations, in fact, were desolating many homes. However, the room was warm, a fine fire blazed, tea was set out by the hearth. So, sinking gratefully into an arm-chair, Henry prepared for a little family gossip.

He was a handsome man in his own way, fairly tall, well set up, strongly built. His colouring was unusual, for he had fair hair, straight and thick, with a gleam in it, and a fair complexion, but his eyes were dark brown. Clearly this was a family trait, for the same combination was found in his sister, who stood now beside him, looking down affectionately at him. She too was tall and well built. Her hair was slightly wavy and showed definitely golden, where Henry's, kept closely cut and smoothly brushed, appeared rather darker. Her eyes, larger and softer than his, were beautiful, and gave colour to her whole face. While neither was, perhaps, strikingly handsome, yet both were unusual in appearance and distinctly pleasing. Brother and sister appeared to be on friendly terms, as was indicated by the way in which Henry spoke.

"Well, Anne," he began, "it's nice to see you again. I'm sorry to be late. I got kept at the office, and couldn't get along here earlier."

"We thought something of the sort had happened," returned his sister placidly. "But we were all so busy getting off our parcels we were quite glad you were behind time. Now they're nearly all done, and we can have our tea in great peace and comfort."

At this juncture they were interrupted by Doreen, Henry's wife, who had been busy at the table behind them, and who came towards her husband, holding out a book.

"Now, Henry, before I send off Aunt Agnes's book you really must write her name in it. Here it is—just scribble a line!"

"Oh heavens, don't start pestering me at once," replied Henry, half vexed, half good-humouredly. "I want a bit of peace first. Don't start harassing me at once. Why can't you write her name in it? It's all the same really."

"Not *at all* the same," answered his wife promptly. "You know Aunt Agnes infinitely prefers to have something from you, and she knows the difference between our writings. And you know she loves those absurd old quotations you always put in to amuse her. Come now, Henry! I've bought the book, and I'll do it up—just be an angel and scribble something in."

Realizing that peace was most quickly attained by prompt action, Henry demurred no further, but, extracting his fountain-pen from his breast-pocket, he took the book his wife held out and, balancing it on his knee, began to inscribe in it an elaborate greeting for his aunt.

His wife stood watching him triumphantly, her pretty, rather silly little face expressing her pleasure in this small victory. She did not, on careful consideration, seem exactly the wife one might have expected such a man as Henry Godfrey to choose. He was clearly intelligent, with an active brain, and probably a good many interests in life. She was pretty enough—smart, and made the most of herself—but there was weakness bordering on silliness in her mouth and expression. She looked an empty-headed, vapid little thing by the side of her sister-in-law, and her looks and charms were not of a sufficiently high order quite to explain why Godfrey had married her.

Something of the sort was perhaps passing through the mind of Anne herself as she stood looking down on them both; on Doreen's neat dark head, now pressed close to Henry's shoulder as she leant from the arm of his chair where she had perched herself. For a faintly contemptuous smile hovered round Anne's mouth, and a slight sigh issued from her lips, as if she thought this little scene typical, and not altogether to her taste.

While Henry's pen travelled swiftly over the title-page, his beautifully neat, tiny writing being the subject of admiring comments from his wife, Mrs. Dutton herself came into the room.

She, though grey-haired and faded, had the same clear dark eyes as her nephew and niece, and the remains of what had once been the same bright complexion. Theirs was an example of a type of looks which, arising in a family, persists from one generation to another, and where the portraits of the grandfather as a boy might be taken for those of the son.

She was carrying in her hands a little tray laden with a covered muffin dish, and, smiling at her nephew, she first stood the dish on the tea-table, and then turned to him to say cheerfully:

"Well, Henry, I heard you come in, so I brought up the muffins. How nice to see you again! I haven't had you here for a long time. Anne," turning to her niece, "will you make the tea now. I think we're all ready for it."

Anne went to the fireplace, and lifting the kettle from the brass hob, where it had been simmering and hissing, put it on to the fire to bring it definitely to the boil.

Mrs. Dutton sat down in the comfortable chair facing Henry, with the low tea-table between them. The red and gold tea-set, bright silver teapot, the covered dish with its hint of excellent, hot, buttery muffins, a delicacy and a custom only fully relished by those who go through our cold, inclement winter season, all combined to emphasize the pleasures of tea-time in December.

The very likeness which showed itself in three of the four faces round the table added another note of comfort. Here were members of one family, all bound together apparently not only by ties of blood but of affection. The idea of harmony, of solidarity, of something more than simple friendship seemed to find expression here.

While they waited for the kettle to be pronounced truly boiling, Anne, sitting back on her heels on the hearthrug, spoke over her shoulder to her brother, who, after a brief nod of acquiescence from his aunt, had resumed his inscription.

"Henry, Doreen has been telling us about this possibility of you going to Germany—"

She broke off abruptly, for, at this moment, all were startled by a sound coming from above.

These converted flats, originally built as good, solid, family mansions, possessed the one great advantage of being fairly sound-proof, or, as the Scots say, "well-deafened." Usually nothing was heard by the occupants of one flat of those above or below. It was therefore the more noticeable when there came at this juncture a muffled thud from immediately above their heads. Indeed, as the room seemed for a moment to quiver, all looked up at the ceiling, and Henry's pen, which he still held, slipped from his fingers to the floor. He reached for it with an impatient exclamation, but glancing at the open book on his knee, and seeing that no smudge or damage had resulted, he calmly proceeded to complete his inscription.

But his wife interrupted him at once. "Oh, Henry!" she exclaimed, laying her hand on his shoulder and glancing upwards, as if she expected something to fall down upon them. "Whatever was that?"

"Old Ewing throwing the furniture about," answered Henry promptly." He's enraged at that nurse he's got, staying out shopping." For gossip filters easily from one flat to the other, and from one member of a family to another, and the ways of the Ewing ménage were familiar to him by repute. "Awful temper that old tartar's got, really," he continued, pensively gazing at his handiwork. "And I dare say—"

But here Doreen Godfrey interrupted him again.

"Oh! be *quiet*, Henry! Don't try to be so funny!" she snapped." Listen! Whatever can they be doing up there?"

She held up her hand to enforce her words, and for a moment they all paused and were silent. Even Mrs. Dutton laid down her piece of muffin and looked upwards. The ceiling was still quivering slightly, making the electric lamps suspended from it sway quite distinctly.

The effect was so strange that Doreen's grip tightened on Henry's arm, in the effort to ensure his stillness. Her husband, however, shook her off impatiently, and glanced quite angrily at his aunt and sister, as if vexed at their continued immobility. The vibration soon ceased, however, and no further sound came from above. There was no movement perceptible at all, in fact, neither footsteps, nor the moving of a chair, nor the scraping of furniture across the floor. Complete silence reigned.

The spell was broken by the kettle, which chose this moment to boil over, and as Anne bent hastily forward to snatch it off the fire her aunt, roused by the movement, spoke.

"Dear me!" she said in a tone of mild surprise, "that *was* a crash. I wonder if Mr. Ewing could have pulled over one of his cabinets? He so often opens them, and gets bits of his collection out in the evening, and goes through them. It sounded to me as if one of those big cabinets might have fallen over. Do you think that could be so?"

"Oh, well," replied Anne, now preparing to pour out the tea, "even if it has, I don't suppose he's hurt, and it will give him something to do to pick up the pieces!"

"Dear me! How unsympathetic you are, Anne!" exclaimed her sister-in-law, rather spitefully. "Why, the poor old thing may have had it fall on him."

"I don't think of him as a poor old thing," retorted Anne, her cheeks, already flushed by the heat of the fire, colouring more deeply with annoyance at Doreen's tone. "I don't think he deserves any pity. He has that nurse there to look after him, too, if he wants any help. Selfish, self-indulgent old man! Coddling himself up with a trained nurse!"

"Well, dear," interrupted Mrs. Dutton, "he really does need that nurse. He's quite crippled now, with his arthritis. Some days he can't even walk, and quite often he has to stay in bed. These are service flats, you know, and he'd have no one to look after him if it weren't for the nurse."

"Yes, I dare say," put in Doreen, rather impertinently, something having evidently caused her to change sides; "but you know, Aunt Mary, I think I agree with Anne there. He is appallingly selfish. Penelope Fordham," with a sideways glance, first at her husband and then at Anne, "is one of our great friends, you know, and it always makes us quite furious to know how miserably she and George live, while old Mr. Ewing doesn't deny himself anything, and lives in perfect luxury, spending heaven knows what on himself. Isn't that true, Henry?"

"That's not our business," said Mrs. Dutton, rather reprovingly, and, as if aware of undercurrents, and wishful to leave this subject, she added, turning to her nephew: "But, Henry, do you think anything is wrong up there? Do you think one of us should go up to see? Perhaps we ought just to run up and inquire?"

"Good heavens, no!" replied Henry crossly. "Whatever makes you suggest such a thing? I must say I agree with Anne. I really detest that selfish old fish, and I certainly don't see why we should concern ourselves with him. Probably he's just knocked over a chair, or a picture's fallen down and smashed."

Doreen, as though suddenly realizing from his irritation that her husband wanted to enjoy some peace and quiet after his day at the office, and repenting the provocation she had given, now glanced imploringly at her aunt, but Mrs. Dutton, intent on her own ideas, never noticed the unspoken signal.

"But it seemed to me rather a loud thump," she went on. "And I'm not sure if Nurse Edwards is back yet. She often goes out for her walk about this time. It would be dreadful if anything had fallen on Mr. Ewing; he's so crippled he's not able to look after himself like anyone else. I think, perhaps, Henry," turning to the only male present, with a cheerful reliance on his capacity and willingness, "that it might be better if you just went up to inquire."

Henry's face had grown positively red with vexation as his aunt gently mused aloud, but, as she gazed with mild but infuriating appeal towards him, he broke out in temper which, even as he spoke, grew more and more uncontrollable.

"Oh, Aunt Mary, for goodness' sake don't fuss like this! I've had a grilling day at the office, and I want a bit of peace! I tell you I'm sure everything's all right up there. There's no need for *us* to bother ourselves. They've just knocked something over and now they've picked it up. Even if one of his beastly pictures has fallen off the wall, what on earth does it matter? I only hope old Ewing cuts his fingers on the glass!"

Catching sight of his aunt's face of amazement at his outburst, Henry checked himself, and then, fuming still, turned on his wife, who was frowning at him from the other side of the hearth. Before he could carry the war into that camp, however, Anne intervened decisively.

"Well, all right, Henry; don't get into such a fuss yourself. I agree with you; I don't think any of us need go dashing up. If Mr. Ewing wants any help he has only to telephone down to the porter. He's not too lame to get to the telephone, you know." The last words she addressed apologetically to her aunt, who, meekly accepting the views of the majority, and seeing the evident wish of her guests to get on with the business of tea, said no more. She stooped to reach up the muffin dish from the hearth, and within a moment or two the little group had settled itself peaceably down.

Yet there was some lingering feeling of constraint or apprehension abroad. For the next few minutes talk seemed to flag; Henry did not regain his amiability, Mrs. Dutton remained rather distrait, Anne rather abrupt. Every member of the party seemed to be unable to give whole-hearted attention to what was going on. No one appeared really to concentrate on the tea and muffins, and it was with that sudden feeling of vague, unreasoning apprehension, crystallizing into definite discomfort, that the silence which had fallen was interrupted by the loud and persistent trilling of the front door bell.

"I'll see who it is," said Anne, who was nearest the door, and rising swiftly to her feet she went out of the room, leaving the door slightly ajar. The others all paused, and then, clear and distinct, they heard an exclamation of horror and surprise.

"Why! Nurse Edwards! Oh! Whatever has happened to you? Poor thing! What *is* the matter?"

A faint murmur followed, and just as Mrs. Dutton rose hastily from her chair, Anne reappeared leading in a woman in nurse's outdoor uniform, but with her face heavily strapped up with plaster and lint, and one arm in a sling. She was a tall, strongly built young woman, the type of one who was well able to cope with all the fatigues and labours of a nurse's life. Indeed, as Mr. Ewing was often rendered so helpless by his illness, he had found it essential to choose as his attendant a young woman of the sturdy, well-developed type. This, incidentally, was far from pleasing to him. He greatly preferred the gentle, mild-eyed, slender woman. Unfortunately, being himself tall, and still quite heavy in spite of his age, and being, therefore, a solid weight to move and manage, he had been obliged, after two or three trials, to abandon his ideal, and fall back on a less ethereal but more robust variety. Partly in consequence of this perpetual slight source of irritation, he tended to vent his secret sense of disappointment by giving way to his moods of bad temper, and in exercising all the petty tyranny which an ailing employer can display towards a paid attendant.

Now, however, the nurse's rather heavy, ruddy face was pale. She looked shaken and nervous, and, to Mrs. Dutton's surprise, her voice trembled slightly as she began:

"I'm so sorry to bother you, Mrs. Dutton; I'm really ashamed to burst in on you like this," with a glance towards Henry and his wife. "But, you see, I've met with an accident—I've been knocked over!"

"By a car?" interrupted Mrs. Dutton anxiously, pushing a chair towards her. "Do sit down. You don't look fit to stand."

The nurse hesitated. Then, as if aware from the kindness of the tone that she really was meeting with sympathy, and might perhaps let herself go a little, she sank down thankfully. For a moment her eyes seemed to brim with tears, and her lips quivered. Evidently she had been badly shaken, and her nerves were thoroughly upset. No one took any notice, and after a scarcely perceptible pause she recovered her self-control and went on to answer the question put to her.

"No, not by a car. Luckily for me, perhaps! In one sense it seems so silly. It was only a bicycle really, but it sent me spinning, and I fell bang against the curb—with all my fairy weight on my arm—" She tried to laugh a little ruefully, as if at her own substantial build, but again sounded slightly hysterical.

"I've had it all done up—it's sprained not broken, and only needed a couple of stitches where I cut the wrist—and I've been trying to hurry back to Mr. Ewing. He'll wonder what on earth I'm up to!"

"Let him wonder!" murmured Doreen, full of sympathy, but quelled at once by an almost fierce look cast by her aunt.

"Oh, I don't want him to be worrying," the nurse hastened to reply. "And I went straight upstairs to the flat when I got back from the hospital, but it's so stupid—it's my right arm I've hurt, and when I got there I couldn't manage to turn the latch-key with my left hand. The key's a bit stiff—so I can't get in!"

"But Mr. Ewing's there!" said Anne in astonishment. "Why, we heard him up there not five minutes ago! Didn't you ring for him to come and let you in?"

"Oh yes, of course I did. Indeed I rang two or three times, but naturally Mr. Ewing didn't know it was me ringing, and he's a great objection to going to the door, lame as he is too, so I suppose he won't bother. Anyhow," rather hastily, as if aware of censure in the air, "he hasn't come to open the door, and I thought if one of you would be so very kind and come up?"

"Why, of course, Nurse," said Mrs. Dutton kindly. "I'll come up with you myself and open the door."

"No, Aunt Mary," interposed Henry. "Don't you bother. I'll go up with Nurse. I'll bear the brunt of breaking the news to Mr. Ewing!"

Mrs. Dutton looked at her nephew and, realizing that his offer was meant to atone for his previous bad-temper, smiled affectionately at him. "Well, that would be very kind of you, Henry, if you're not too tired yourself."

Doreen, who knew better than the others how cross her husband was after what had almost certainly been a worrying day in the city, and that his present amiability to his aunt might change to something different towards her when they should be on the way home, rose uneasily and, pushing herself forward, said: "Don't you worry, Henry; we know you're tired. I'll go up with Nurse."

"Nonsense, Doreen!" said Anne sharply, before Henry could reply. "That's ridiculous. Let Henry go; it won't hurt him to go up one flight of stairs!"

She spoke so vehemently that both Doreen and her aunt gazed at her with some surprise, and poor mild Mrs. Dutton, who felt her tea-party was not turning out at all well, turned, rather aghast, to her nephew, to see how he would take this little outburst. Henry, however, by now appeared to have recovered his temper, or at least his self-control, and he merely smiled quite agreeably at his aunt, repeating: "It's all right, Aunt Mary, I don't mind a bit. Of course I'll go." Reassured, Mrs. Dutton turned to the nurse, who stood there looking rather pale and shaken: "But won't you just stay and have a cup of tea, Nurse? You must need one after an accident, even if it's not a very serious one, and there's no one upstairs to get you one. You can leave Mr. Ewing just a little longer—or Mr. Godfrey will go up and tell him now what has happened."

"No, thank you very much," replied the nurse, clearly impatient to be off. "I've been kept out a long time as it is, and Mr. Ewing will wonder wherever I've got to—I must really get up to him at once—I'd rather, thank you"—this with an anxious glance at Henry.

He, with the obvious determination to do the thing thoroughly, smiled back at her. "Very well, Nurse, come along, and perhaps I'll have a chat with Mr. Ewing while you get yourself some tea up there. I'll quite like to see his collection again, really."

The two went off together, but Anne, turning to her aunt, after a moment's hesitation said: "I think I'll go up too, Aunt Mary. That poor woman looks thoroughly upset, and I don't suppose Mr. Ewing will be in the least sympathetic or considerate. He'll probably just grumble at her for being late. Don't you think I'd better go after them? I can get her some tea, and see she lies down."

But her aunt hesitated. "Mr. Ewing isn't very smooth-tempered, dear. I think you'd better wait a little, and go up, perhaps, after the first commotion is over."

Anne did not answer, but recognizing the force of her aunt's suggestion she moved towards the door rather slowly, and then murmured, as she went out into the hall:

"Yes, you're right. I'll just wait a moment or two, and then slip up and see if I can do anything without seeing him, perhaps."

She paused in the hall, where a blast of cold air, blowing in from the street, told her that her brother had left the front door open behind him. Anne moved rather uneasily down the passage, and went slowly out on to the broad top step, sheltered by the old-fashioned portico beyond. She stood there for a moment, shivering in the raw damp which struck her coming from the warm room, her gaze idly turning to the door of No. 5B, which stood ajar too, and as she gazed she heard footsteps running lightly but swiftly down the stairs within. She did not recognize them as her brother's, but before she had time to collect herself a man came out, not apparently noticing her, for she stood in the shadow cast by one of the stout pillars supporting the porch. He hesitated for a second on the top step, glancing up and down the street. Anne subconsciously thought he was shrinking from the plunge into the cold and damp, a feeling experienced by those who must adventure out from the warmth into a thoroughly wet night. Before she could begin to connect him with anything in the flat above he had run quickly down the steps, and, walking very swiftly, he vanished down the street, holding his coat collar closely together round his chin as he went.

Vaguely reassured by a gesture so homely and prosaic, and realizing that all seemed peaceful in the flat above—no sound of angry voice nor exclamations—Anne turned back to tell the others she thought they had vexed Henry without cause, and that Mr. Ewing had taken Nurse's adventure quite peaceably, but even as she reached the passage within she stopped dead, for bursting out above came shriek upon shriek, followed by the thud of flying feet coming down the stairs. As she rushed instantly back towards the portico, the sounds came towards her.

Horrified, she beheld Nurse Edwards, her face ghastly, her veil awry, stumbling frantically down, crashing wildly against the wall with her injured arm, apparently oblivious to what she was doing. She flung herself towards Anne, who, rushing forward, tried to catch her and restrain her desperate flight. The only effect she produced as she clutched at the swaying figure was apparently to add to the woman's terror. As Anne's firm grip seized her sound arm, she lost all self-control and, screaming and uttering wild peal upon peal of laughter, collapsed in violent hysterics at Anne's feet.

Helpless until someone could come to her assistance, and calling loudly to Doreen and her aunt, Anne glanced frantically up at the next staircase, just visible from where she stood, hoping to see her brother appear. Doreen and her aunt, she felt, would be inadequate helpers, and she needed Henry's strength to carry the woman in. But no sound came from above, and no Henry appeared.

Chapter IV

THE RETURN

Stealthy guests have secret watchwords, private entrances.

The Other Half-Rome, R. BROWNING.

When Henry Godfrey came out of his aunt's flat with Nurse Edwards, they turned towards the entrance of 5B. The main door was ajar, as indeed Nurse had left it when she came down from her fruitless attempt to get in.

Brought up to "leave gates as you find them", he once more left it slightly open, and, rather slowly, to suit his evidently exhausted companion, began to mount the staircase which led to Simon Ewing's maisonette. No. 5B occupied the first and second floors, and above that again was the top floor containing flats 5C and D, at present unoccupied. The staircase went straight to the first landing, where Mr. Ewing's front door directly faced anyone coming up. There was a light on the landing, which lit up the door quite distinctly. As these flats were part of a converted house, their front doors were not very substantial, and, in order to make their front lobbies brighter in the daytime, had thick panels of frosted glass let in to their upper halves.

As they came to a standstill before the door, and while his companion began to fumble with her left hand for the latch key in her bag, he looked idly about him, and, seeing her trembling fingers, spoke to her with greater softness and kindness than he had hitherto shown.

"Let me find the key for you, Nurse. It's difficult for you with your bad hand." And as he took the bag she willingly relinquished, he paused before opening it and added, his eyes on her pale face:

"You look rather badly knocked about, Nurse. I wonder they let you come home?"

"Oh, well, Mr. Godfrey, I'm not really badly hurt. I'm more bruised than anything, though my arm's sprained and my wrist and face cut. The doctor at the hospital sent me back in a taxi, and he says I'm to go to bed, and in the morning get Dr. Ainslie from opposite to have a look at me."

Henry had been looking compassionately at her, but now, as if recalled to the sense that the sooner she was in bed the better, he extracted the key from the bag, following her directions as to the compartment it was in, turned briskly towards the door, and began to insert the key into the latch.

As he did so he spoke, over his shoulder, feeling perhaps that he should prepare the woman for a rather stormy reception.

"It's very unlucky for you, and I don't know, but I am afraid that there may have been some little mishap here. We heard rather a crash up here while we were at tea, as if something had been knocked over."

"Oh dear!" responded the nurse, with dismay. "I do hope not! Mr. Ewing always gets rather vexed if I'm kept out late and leave him too long alone, and if anything *has* gone wrong he'll not have been able to put it to rights by himself."

Clearly forgetting her own misfortunes in the apprehensions as to what her employer might have to add to his sense of injury, she pressed forward, and, as Henry opened the door and stepped aside, she went quickly into the flat before him.

She hesitated for the fraction of a second, and then went across the little hall in the direction of an open door from which light shone out. As she did so she turned and held up her finger to Henry, as if to beg him to stand still for a moment and give her time to go in and bear the brunt of any storm that might be about to break.

Henry obeyed her injunction, and stood still; and at this very instant a man came quietly down the narrow staircase at the back, leading to the part of the maisonette above. Mr. Ewing's flat was composed of the middle floors of the original house, and though his drawing-room and bedroom were large, good rooms, on what was meant to be the first floor, the rooms above were very much smaller. The staircase which gave access to his upper part was simply the old back stairs of the house, now thrown open into the first floor. It was therefore of a different type from the big main stair, and was really only a narrow, wooden flight emerging at the dark farther end of the former first-floor landing, or the lobby as it was now called. The light in the hall itself was lit, but not the light for the upper stair; and consequently the man, coming down in the shadow, was not perceptible until he had actually reached the bottom of the flight and was coming across the little hall.

He advanced rather quickly, putting on a soft felt hat, which he had been holding in his hand, as he came, pulling it down low over his face and turning up his collar—evidently in preparation for meeting the cold, wet night outside.

Nurse Edwards had turned back at the sound of his footsteps crossing the marble floor of the lobby, and for a brief moment she stood still, watching him walk towards the door. She said nothing, and Godfrey accordingly stood quiet too. As the man reached the door, almost brushing past Godfrey, he nodded a good night in a pleasant sort of manner. Then, as soon as he was outside the flat, he walked quickly across the outer landing and disappeared swiftly and quietly down the stairs.

Henry hesitated, wondering, as he afterwards said, whether perhaps he ought to have called after the man to know if all was well;

but the nurse, having glanced after the retreating figure, turned rather slowly towards the drawing-room, paused, as if uncertain how best to present herself in her battered and dishevelled condition, and then pushed the door open and went in.

Henry followed close on her heels. At first the room, to both his and her evident surprise, seemed empty. The lights were on, the fire blazing brightly, and there was no occupant visible. But the nurse, advancing round the centre table towards the fireplace, where stood the big invalid chair, was brought to a sudden standstill. Struck by her attitude and downward gaze, Henry instantly hurried forward. She was looking, in a dull bewilderment, at a confused heap upon the ground. A big rug was lying crumpled up—at least it seemed to be a rug.

With a sudden violent thudding of the heart Henry bent down, touched the rug, then twitched it aside. At the sight of what lay beneath, his breath seemed to leave his body. For a second or two both man and woman stood paralysed, and then the woman, wildly flinging her uninjured arm before her face, rushed headlong from the room and down the stairs, hoarse screams pouring from her throat as she ran.

The lifting of the rug had uncovered what Henry subconsciously knew must be the body of a man; but the awful, muddled heap, with pools of blood soaking into the carpet round it, at first brought to his horrified senses no clear conception whatever. Something, once alive—now dead, was the limit of what his brain, in its whirling and reeling, seemed to grasp. Then he felt as if he too would lose all self-control and break out into wild shrieking, as, from that blood-stained tangle, something seemed to protrude and move.

Sweating with anguish, he forced himself to drop to his knees and peer more closely. He saw then that the faint movement came from the fingers of one hand, lying upon a blood-stained breast. But, even as he grasped that fact, he understood that it was only the spark of a dying fire. Life might have lingered for a moment in that battered frame, but as he looked he knew that the moment had passed.

Half an hour had gone since the discovery of the crime. Henry and Anne Godfrey were efficient people, and in that brief period everything possible had been done.

Anne had eventually, with the help of her aunt and Doreen, got the distraught Nurse Edwards into their flat and into her aunt's bed. Mrs. Dutton, while overcome with horror, kept her head, and was ready to do anything she could for the poor creature. Without either of them understanding, from the incoherent, gasping words which were all she could utter, what had happened, both realized that the fall and crash had signified that something terrible had happened to the old man above. The immediate necessity was to get help, and Doreen was sent flying across the road to fetch Dr. Ainslie, with instructions to impress upon him that something was very seriously wrong and that he must come at once. Then, leaving her aunt to deal with the nurse, Anne hastened up the staircase which led to Mr. Ewing's flat. As she ran panting into the little lobby, Henry came out of the drawing-room. His ghastly pallor and look of shock and fear roused in Anne a sense of something appalling, which increased to utter terror as her eyes fell upon his hand, stretched out to push her back.

"Go away, go away, Anne!" hurriedly and urgently he muttered, advancing towards her, and waving her back towards the staircase.

"Henry! Henry! your hand! oh, look at it!"

Startled, he glanced down, and then, snatching out his handkerchief, began to wipe the sticky blood from his fingers.

"Oh, I know! I know! Don't *talk* about it, don't *look* at it!" he murmured, his whole face convulsed and twisted. "Oh, it's too awful! Anne! Come on, come down! I must fetch the police at once." He began to stumble as quickly as he could towards the street, and Anne realized that he was on the verge of fainting. She gave one glance back towards the lobby, where the soft, bright lights and open doors, showing only glimpses of lighted rooms, seemed but the more frightening by reason of the glitter and silence. Then, leaving the lobby door still well open behind them, she followed her brother down the stairs.

Out on the porch he paused to draw in some deep breaths of the cold, raw air. Here, in contrast to the brightly lit rooms above, was the rain soaking steadily down, and the murky, fog-wreathed street. Anne felt she must not speak, she must wait for her brother to regain his self-control. Exercising all her own, she stood quietly beside him. After only a moment or two, he put back the handkerchief with which he had continued to wipe and scrub his hand, and, turning a very ashy face towards her, he said, quite firmly:

"Anne, Mr. Ewing has been murdered. We must get the police and the doctor."

"I've already sent for Dr. Ainslie," replied Anne promptly. "That poor nurse needs him at once."

"Nurse Edwards! Where is she? I forgot all about her."

"In Aunt Mary's bedroom," replied Anne briefly; and, taking her brother by the arm, she drew him towards their aunt's door. "Come in and telephone for the police, Henry. You'll have to do that. I couldn't tell them what they'll want to know." She had turned to go with him; then, a sudden thought striking her, she paused, and, while Henry made for the telephone in Mrs. Dutton's sitting-room, she stood hesitating. She had remembered that open door above. Thoughts flashed through her. "Murder"—therefore a murderer. Had he gone? Was he still up there? She remembered the top flat of all was empty, the staircase unlit. Someone might have run up there to hide! Then, like a blaze of lightning, came the recollection of the man who had come down and out, before ever Nurse had begun to shriek. A feeling of violent relief ran through her. "That was the man, and he's gone—he's not up there—we are safe from him!" Yet again some instinct made her hesitate to go inside her aunt's door, passionately though she longed to be with other human beings, not alone, outside that terrifying door leading up to unknown things. *One* man had gone—true—but suppose there were another? She realized it was her duty to stay where she was, able to see if anyone should come down the stair, to wait, at any rate, until some sort of help should come. So, for a few moments, which seemed unending, she stood still in the shadow of the portico, until, with a relief which brought the sweat out into the palms of her hands, she heard voices break out from across the road, and saw Dr. Ainslie, accompanied by Doreen and by another man, coming hurrying across towards her.

"Oh, Dr. Ainslie!" she cried, "go in quickly to Henry! It's dreadful—Mr. Ewing's dead, Henry says he's been murdered—and his nurse has had an accident. You'll find her in our flat—but *please*," and she turned imploringly towards the strange man, "stay here till the police come. There may still be someone—the murderer—up there! We haven't been in to look!" and she pointed towards the doorway and staircase of the upper flat.

Utterly dumbfounded, doctor and stranger gazed at her. Then both instinctively started towards Mr. Ewing's doorway. She checked them, laying her hand on the arm of the man, who stood nearest.

"No, don't go in; he might be still in Mr. Ewing's flat, or he might be hiding on the stairs above ready to rush down if you went into the flat. And the police will be here directly—don't, don't go up!—and oh, doctor," turning to him, "that poor woman must be seen to—she's all collapsed from the shock, coming on top of her accident. I don't know *what's* happened—or what Henry and she have seen up there!"

Dr. Ainslie, startled afresh by this appeal, at once turned towards Mrs. Dutton's entrance, leaving Anne with the stranger. He, realizing apparently the sense of what she had been saying, stood beside her for a moment, looking intently inwards towards the light faintly gleaming down the empty staircase. Then, as if recalled to the girl beside him and to the need to reassure her if possible, he turned his face towards her and said politely: "You are living here, I think? I am your new neighbour opposite. Hetherington is my name."

"Oh yes," responded Anne, feeling bound to make some effort to maintain this normal note; "I'm staying here with my aunt. Mr. Hetherington? Why, I think I saw your canvasses and things going in a day or two ago." She was vaguely feeling that it would only be polite to inquire if he were the Mr. Hetherington who had recently held a one-man show of landscapes, when the sound of a motor coming fast along the street caused her to break off. With the utmost thankfulness she saw the car draw up in front of No. 5, and realized that the men emerging from it were the police. She felt that she could really bear no more, now that authority had come to take over responsibility. She was conscious that her legs suddenly felt as if they would give way beneath her, and intent only on returning to her own family, she no longer gave one further look towards Mr. Hetherington, who, apparently resolving not to miss the sensational happenings which the next ten minutes must bring, remained sturdily planted on the steps.

Of the occupants of the car, now disembarked and advancing towards her, the one who came ahead was Detective-Inspector Woods, the C.I.D. man attached to the district. London police stations now have each a small corps of C.I.D. men working with them, and when a crime occurs in a London area it is these C.I.D. men who are dispatched to the scene. Thus, unlike the provinces, Scotland Yard is automatically called to the spot in the persons of these special men.

"No. 5B, madam?" inquired the inspector.

"Yes! Yes!" said Anne, recognizing that here was the official force. "It's murder, I'm afraid. My brother's been up. We live in the flat below.

He says Mr. Ewing of No. 5B has been killed! He—my brother—can tell you all about it. But oh," as the men started towards the entry, "wait a minute—someone ought to stay here; that staircase leads to the little empty flats above, as well as to Mr. Ewing's, and someone may be hiding up there."

The inspector nodded, understanding the importance of what she said. A few brief inquiries of Anne, and some low-toned words to his subordinates, and then, stationing two men below at the entry, he started up the staircase to No. 5B, leaving Anne to return to her own premises.

As he mounted the stairs Woods was aware that he was stiffening himself in preparation for whatever he might find in the flat above. For, experienced as he was, he knew that no man's nerves are altogether proof when brought face to face with the physical remains of the victim of a murder. Contrary, perhaps, to general belief, a policeman has nerves which shrink from the sight of violence just as much as those of other men.

In person Woods was a tall, handsome man, between the ages of thirty and forty. He had a thin, intellectual stamp of face, dark hair, very bright, dark-blue eyes. He looked neither hard nor unapproachable. His calm, efficient, quiet manner inspired confidence, while something lurking in the character of his gaze, and in the lines of his mouth, showed that he possessed the invaluable gift of being firm without being autocratic. Here was a man to investigate and to probe, and yet without rousing antagonism. He had a certain reputation, and one which was partly based upon the extreme thoroughness and tenacity with which he would scrutinize every detail of a crime.

He noted, therefore, as he went up, that the landing beside Mr. Ewing's front door was well lighted, and that the panels of glass on each side of the door allowed anyone outside to see if the flat within were lighted up.

The outer lobby here, before the modern entrance to the flat, was still fairly broad, for the house had originally been a large one, planned with spacious landings and a wide staircase. In order to reach the topmost door of all, which was arranged in two of those minute affairs politely called "flatlets", but which were really little more than "one-room flats", the main stairs went on up, rounding a corner and winding away out of sight. Owing to the smallness of the rooms and poor accommodation they offered, there had been no demand for these flatlets, and they had remained unlet.

Noting briefly that it would have been extremely easy for anyone to have been lurking on this open staircase, out of sight round the corner, and going up a short way to discover, as he had expected, that there were no bulbs in the electric lights on that part of the stairs, Woods turned back, and at length approached the threshold of No. 5B.

The door itself stood wide open as Henry Godfrey had left it.

Dispatching two men to go on and search the approach to the empty flats above, Woods was just entering the lobby when he heard the clatter of steps behind him, and turning, saw with pleasure that the police surgeon had arrived, together with the photographer and extra helpers who had been assembled and dispatched from the station.

"Glad you've come, Doctor," he exclaimed. "I've not been in yet, nor anyone else, so you and I will be the first on the field. No one has touched the body, I understand."

They had paused for a moment in the hall while Woods instructed the photographers and print experts to set to work at once on the front door, inside and out, and the doctor began hurriedly to undo the clasps of his case.

"No one else here?" said the doctor. "Well, that's good. Who is it who's been murdered?"

"I understand it is an old gentleman, Mr. Simon Ewing, living alone."

"No relations here, then?" glancing swiftly as he spoke at the beautiful decorations of the hall around them.

"No, no relations. He lived alone, and this is a service flat so there were no maids. Beyond a Mr. Godfrey, who found the body and notified the station, no one has been near. We'd better go in now and see how things are."

The door to their left was open and showed the lighted room within, clearly the chief sitting-room of the flat. Beyond, another door was visible, and at the far end the small service stair could be seen, running down from the dark regions above.

It's in here, I expect," said Woods briefly, pointing to the open door. Leading the way, he went in, glanced round, and then moved at once towards the hearth. He stooped and lifted aside the rug which Henry had replaced over the body.

Repressing the exclamation which rose to his lips, he stood aside to make way for the doctor.

I'll just wait for you to tell me, Doctor," he said, with lips which despite himself seemed suddenly to have gone stiff. "Though I can see for myself, of course, this *is* a murder, there's no doubt of that."

Dr. Carr muttered something inaudible, as he in his turn saw what lay before them. Then, kneeling down beside the body, he began his examination.

"Dead, of course," he said at once, and glanced at his watch to note the time. "Difficult to tell you much with all this mess, and I take it you don't want me to move the body—nothing to be done *for* him, poor fellow."

Woods made no reply. Indeed for the moment he was filled only with an unprofessional longing to get away from the sight which was filling him with revulsion and horror. To steady himself he switched his attention away from the body, and began to consider the other aspects of his task. He remembered that the girl he had found at the door below had told him her brother had information for him, and he determined to run down and hear at once what these people could tell him.

"Doctor, I'll leave you for a moment. I want to interview someone below. You'll not need me just now, and I'll be back directly."

The doctor nodded agreement, without speaking, and Woods ran hurriedly down the stairs. His subordinate, Sergeant Riley, was standing on the front steps, and at the sight of Woods advanced towards him.

"Who are these people at No. 5A?" inquired the inspector." I hear they've something to tell us."

"Mrs. Dutton occupies the flat," replied Riley, "but I've made a few inquiries, and it was her nephew, Mr. Henry Godfrey, who gave the alarm and, as I understand, found the body."

"Well," said Woods, "we'd better perhaps see him first, and find out what he has to say."

Chapter V

THE DEAD

By the utmost exercise of violence, made safe and sure by craft.

The Other Half-Rome, R. BROWNING.

As Woods and Riley entered Mrs. Dutton's flat, Henry himself advanced to meet them.

"Thank heaven you've come, Inspector!" he exclaimed. "This is a most awful business—" He was interrupted by the sound of hysterical shrieks from the next room, and, in answer to the inspector's questioning glance, went on: "That's Mr. Ewing's nurse, poor girl. She'd met with an accident earlier in the evening, and most unfortunately for her, she and I discovered the body. It's upset her altogether, and the doctor's with her now."

The inspector nodded, to show that he realized both the condition of the woman, and the fact that he must wait for any evidence she might have to give until the hysteria had been dealt with.

"Now, sir, just tell me as briefly as you can how you made the discovery. I want to know exactly when you went up, who went with you, and who has been up since. When I know that I can go back myself and get on with things."

"Well," said Henry, "I don't live here. This is my aunt's flat. My wife and I were here to tea. Soon after 5 o'clock Nurse Edwards came in. She is a trained nurse who looks after Mr. Ewing, as he is badly crippled with arthritis. His is the flat above this—maisonette rather—he has two floors. She—Nurse Edwards—had met with an accident while she was out, and had hurt her arm. She asked that someone should come up and open the door of the flat for her. I went up, unlocked the door with her key; we went in together, and found Mr. Ewing dead. His body was lying in the front room. Nurse went into hysterics, and rushed straight down here. I saw there was nothing to be done, so came away to give the alarm. No one has been up since."

"No one been up since?" queried Woods sharply. "How do you know that, sir? You yourself rang up the station, I understand?"

"Yes," said Henry, aware that his statement, which he had purposely made as brief as possible, required amplifying, "that is so. But my sister, hearing the nurse rushing down, came out to meet her, and when I came down and in here to telephone, she remained outside in the porch to watch and see that no one went in."

Woods mentally paid a tribute to the girl who had undertaken such a job, but, anxious to make sure of his ground, inquired: "Can I see the lady, sir?"

"Why, yes," and going to the door Henry called: "Anne, would you come? The inspector wants you a moment."

A brief scrutiny of the girl who entered soon convinced Woods that he might rely on anything she told him. Anne's composure, the firm lines of her pale face, the steadiness of her voice, convinced him that, whatever her inward feelings might be, she had not allowed any nervousness or dread to drive her within her own home for shelter.

"Yes," she replied, in answer to his question. "I went up to see if I could help my brother, but met him coming down. While he came in here, I stood in the porch. I stood there alone, from the moment my brother and I came out, until the doctor and Mr. Hetherington from opposite came across. Then Mr. Hetherington and I stood there until the police car came. No one came out of the upstairs flats after my brother and the nurse came down."

As the inspector nodded and turned towards the door, she added, with an irrepressible gasp, and in a voice which she could not succeed in keeping quite normal and steady:

"But someone had come down before that! Before the nurse had called out, I mean."

Thunderstruck, the inspector and Riley gazed at her, and she added quickly: "A man had come out just before."

"Oh! Good God!" came from Henry in a burst, and, like a flash, Woods turned on him.

"Did you see the man, sir?"

"Yes, I did." And Henry's horrified tone showed that to him, as to Anne, came the realization that he had probably set eyes on the murderer in the act of leaving the scene of a crime. "Of course I did! He came down the stairs from the top of the house, and he nodded 'Good night' to me as he went out and down the staircase to the street."

"But you mean you saw him and didn't stop him? Didn't question him?" broke from Woods.

"No, I didn't. I never thought there was anything wrong. He looked all right—and the nurse didn't say anything—I thought she knew him. Why should I have stopped him? I didn't know of the murder!" Henry's agitation made him almost incoherent.

"The nurse?" queried Woods. "Did she see him too?"

"Yes," answered Henry. "She and I went into the flat together, and she was going into the drawing-room when we saw the man. He came down those stairs that lead up to the top rooms."

At this moment Mrs. Dutton came out of her back bedroom into the hall, and as she opened the door of her room the sound of violent sobbing was audible, mixed with the murmur of the doctor's voice. The inspector gave a brief ear to the sounds, which evidently convinced him that he could not for the present hope to interview the woman, and turning back to Henry, he inquired:

"You mean that the nurse distinctly saw this man, and did not challenge him?"

"Yes," said Henry, with a disturbed air; "she certainly saw him, and I, naturally, thought he was someone she knew, just a visitor."

"Perhaps he was," suggested Woods. "Surely that must be so. The nurse would have said something, I imagine, if he'd been a stranger. And if he's known to her we shall soon get on his track. Though, of course, we don't know, as yet, that he's anything to do with the crime. Did he seem agitated at all, to your view? Or show any special haste to get away?"

"I don't know," hesitated Henry. "He passed me quite quietly, and he went on down the stairs without any special hurry, I should say. I think, at any rate, he must have been in the drawing-room and *seen* what there was up there," and, at the recollection of what he himself had seen, a violent shudder ran through him.

Woods glanced at him keenly. "Well, sir, I must be off again up there myself, if you've nothing further to add. You saw this man leave the flat; Miss Godfrey here saw him come out of the front door. No one else came out, I understand?" His sharp eyes took in Henry's shake of the head and Anne's affirming gesture.

"Now, Riley," turning to his subordinate, "this is your business. Get a description of this man from Mr. Godfrey and from Miss Godfrey, and see if the doctor can get anything from the nurse. She's the important one, of course. Then come up, as soon as ever you can, and we'll send off to the stations, and get things going to fetch this fellow in. But I needn't tell you to be as quick as you can. We mustn't lose a moment in getting after him."

He spoke decisively, almost cheerfully, for Godfrey's account had taken a weight off his mind. He had little doubt that the man in question was the murderer, who had actually been seen, at close quarters, by three people, and in view of what Godfrey had said, he had even less doubt that the individual in question was someone known to the nurse. Very little time had been lost, and with a name and description, the police ought not to have much difficulty in collecting the fugitive.

He scribbled a brief note for Dr. Ainslie, begging him, as a matter of the utmost urgency, to call in Sergeant Riley as soon as the nurse could be interviewed. This he handed to Anne. "Perhaps you'd take this in to the doctor, Miss Godfrey? If you go in, it won't frighten her as a visit from the sergeant might, and we must get her information as soon as possible."

Leaving her to this task, he once more set out for the scene of the murder itself.

When he re-entered the flat above, the police surgeon was just completing his examination. While Carr scribbled a few notes on the writing-pad which he held upon his knee, Woods began to look more carefully round the beautiful room.

At once it became clear that though a violent murder had been done, there had been no struggle. *Everything* seemed to be in absolute order, not even a chair overturned. A sort of writing-board, which looked as if it had been used, was lying across a high stool, on it a book of stamps, some paper and envelopes, some fragments of string and sealing-wax, showed that the quite peaceable and ordinary occupation of dispatching letters and parcels had been in operation.

Woods mentally added these items to the facts he already knew. "No struggle, no attempt to resist, everything quite tidy and in order. Must have been someone he knew, as I thought from the nurse's behaviour," he mused—again feeling that pleasant sense that his task was to be reassuringly easy.

The big arm-chair had its cushions in place, dented still where the head of the occupant had rested.

Dr. Carr stood up.

"Head battered in, Inspector, as I expect you can see for yourself. There's one very large deep wound here, on the left-hand side, above the ear. That in itself would be fatal. Then there are extensive injuries round the whole of the left side of the head—I should say, roughly, nine or ten blows. The one to the front was the first given, and would be sufficient to cause death. It has penetrated right through the bone and smashed into the brain."

"What sort of instrument do you think was used?"

"Something heavy and sharp—you see, it's cut right through."

"Something very heavy?"

"Fairly heavy, yes."

"How long do you think it would take to inflict these blows?"

"They'd be done very quickly indeed. I should say they would all be inflicted in less than half a minute. I think the first blow was dealt when he was sitting, with the head bent slightly forward, then he'd fall to the ground, and all the others were dealt while he lay on the ground."

Woods indicated the spots and splashes radiating from the body on to the furniture near by.

"Do you think these splashes bear that out?"

"Yes, I do. Look at them closely and you'll see they all radiate from this centre, made by the position of the head. They are all in an upward direction too, showing they splashed up from the floor."

"I suppose the murderer is bound to be heavily spattered too?"

"Well, that I can't say definitely. If he knelt down, of course, he'd be bound to have his face and hair very much splashed."

"And his hands and arms?"

"I think his left hand would be, not the right. You don't, as a rule, find blood so much on the hand that holds the weapon."

"Not if there are a great many blows?"

"No. There would be a great deal of blood on the left, where he'd hold his victim down, but not on the right. I think, as the last blows were struck with the head on the ground, the murderer will have blood on his feet and legs."

"How long does it take for blood to become clotted?"

"It varies a bit. Roughly from five or six to ten minutes. Death took place about half an hour ago. The old man made no great resistance—didn't succeed in rolling away at all."

"How do you know that, Doctor?" said Woods briefly.

Carr glanced down again and nodded towards the carpet. "Blood quite localized," he said, "not a very great deal of it either, considering, and all just round this one place where the head lies. There's nothing more for me to do now. You may as well get your part of the business done."

He turned away, made a few more notes in his book, and then, unable to repress his feelings despite his professional calm, he added: "Disgusting, Woods, utterly disgusting. He's old, he couldn't have had a chance. Hope you catch the devil who did it."

"Well, we've a good deal to go on, Doctor, I believe," replied Woods tersely, for he too felt stirred out of his customary control. "The man was seen by three people, and one of them ought to be able to tell us who he was; she must know him, I think."

"That's good—and I won't keep you from being after him. The sooner he's landed in jail the better," and, really thankful to get away from the horrible scene, Carr moved towards the door.

"That depends on how quickly your colleague can get our witness fit to talk," Woods called after him. "Indeed, Doctor, you might just drop in next door and see if you can help us there?"

But even as he spoke Sergeant Riley came breathlessly up the stairs and in, and one glance at his face showed Woods that matters had gone wrong.

*

"Sir," said Riley, without wasting any time, "I've seen the nurse. She's better, and able to make a statement. The doctor put her the questions I wanted answered. She confirms what Mr. Godfrey says. They both went into the flat together. She saw this man in the hall, but says he was a complete stranger to her, and she can't tell us anything about him."

"What!" exclaimed Woods, horrified at this downfall of his confident expectations. "She didn't know him? But then, why on earth didn't she speak to him and ask who he was?"

Riley shook his head. "I didn't go into all that, sir. She's quite definite she didn't know the man, and says she just thought him a visitor who'd been in to see Mr. Ewing. She's met with an accident herself, sir, to-night, and seems pretty bad with it all, and the doctor says she mustn't be questioned too much."

Woods nodded comprehension, but he felt a pang of dismay. He had been building a good deal on this identification.

"Told Mr. Godfrey this?" he queried.

"Why, yes, sir. I saw him again after taking the nurse's statement. His version is that *he* thought the man was a visitor, and concluded from the nurse taking no notice that he was someone whom she knew came to the house."

The two men stared at each other aghast. Both comprehended that it was in fact quite possible for two individuals to credit each other with knowledge which actually neither possessed. Yet the results seemed incredible.

"Why! To think," exclaimed Riley, as the full meaning of the situation dawned on him, "they must have caught the fellow practically red-handed—if they'd challenged him. Good heavens! To think he walked out past both of them and got away perfectly easily! It's past belief, sir!"

Woods, glancing at the heap before the fireplace, which Riley, standing where he did, had not as yet seen, realized all the more acutely what that man had left, and the iron nerve which must have carried him across that hall and past the man and woman on the threshold. He brushed his hand across his forehead and, with a deepening sense of foreboding, said:

"Couldn't either of them, or that Miss Godfrey, give a description? I imagine they saw him close to, and in a good light."

Riley shook his head.

"The nurse only saw him from behind. She says she'd gone across towards the drawing-room, and was standing in the doorway, and she looked back and watched him walk across the lobby. She can only say he was fairly tall, thin, and, she thinks, young."

"What does Mr. Godfrey say?" asked Woods." He was facing him, and the hall light was on; he *must* be able to tell us fairly accurately."

"No," returned Riley, "he's no more use to us than the nurse. He says the man was putting on his hat and turning up his coat collar. He never saw the face distinctly at all. Just had a general impression. Someone about 5 feet 10 or 11. Slim, youngish—under forty-five he'd say—fairish, he *thinks*, but can't really say for certain—dressed in a raincoat and a soft hat. No, sir, Miss Godfrey's the one who gave me the best description. She saw him, of course, in the portico, close to. She says the man paused on the front step and looked up and down the street. She saw him quite distinctly as there's a street lamp on the pavement at the very foot of the steps. She gives his age as about thirty-five, thin, thin-faced, dark, with a slight moustache and spectacles. Wearing a soft felt hat, grey, and a light raincoat. Mr. Godfrey corroborates colour of the coat and hat."

For a moment Woods visualized the figure these words called up. Actually he had a despairing certainty that the description was of very little value—it was both too vague and would fit too many men in a great city. However, for the moment it was all he had to go on, and he must make the best of it.

"Well, go down to the station, Riley, and get the description made out, and all posts notified. Ask if anyone in the locality saw any such person, at 5 o'clock or thereabouts. Ask especially for anyone answering the description seen running, or showing haste anywhere, either in shops or on the tubes and undergrounds. Cool as he was, he must have wanted to get as far away from here as he could, in as short a time as possible. He mayn't have kept up that pose of calm much farther than beyond the street corner. Circularize all the shops where he might, or may in future, try to buy new clothes. Anyway, do the best you can, and be quick. Time's the best factor we have on our side now."

He turned away, all his former confidence gone, for he realized now how far more difficult was the task before him. Instinctively he braced himself to take even more meticulous notice of every detail of the scene he had now to examine.

The photographers were only awaiting his instructions to set to work. Immediately on his signal they began. Photographs of the body as it lay, of the room from various angles, of the objects on the bureau, were to be taken. Woods, who had entered and briefly examined the other rooms, bade them take shots of lobby and bedrooms. Until these had been obtained, nothing was to be moved, everything to remain in place as it had been found. The front door showed no signs whatever of having been tampered with. In every room all seemed to be in order, though Woods's keen eye had detected something in one of the top rooms which he had not expected. Waiting to deal with that, he hurried on the work of the photographers, eager to get the fingerprint men to work. Every member of the group apparently was struck with the absolute order and neatness of each place they entered.

A brief search of Mr. Ewing's bedroom revealed nothing whatever. There were no signs of disturbance or disorder. The room retained its air of peaceful luxury, the room of a semi-invalid, who spent a good deal of his time in bed, and who had surrounded himself with every contrivance to make himself comfortable.

The inspector and his companion, after a thorough search, went on up the narrow staircase to the upper rooms. Woods paused to tell the fingerprint men to be sure to test the banister-rail and the electric-light switches most carefully, in the hope that the man, in coming down, had inadvertently let his hand rest on the rail.

Above them were only three smallish rooms. One was occupied by the nurse, one was a bathroom, and one a spare-room. In the bathroom there were no signs of anyone having washed. The soap was dry, and the towel quite dry too.

Actually the spare-room was more in the nature of a box-room, for it was clearly never used. A handsome old mahogany bed with head and foot boards, but with no bedding on it, stood against one wall, and scattered about the room were the other pieces of a very handsome old bedroom suite, but there were no signs that the room was ever occupied. The bare dressing-table and great mirror had a blank, cold look. A few trunks and boxes were piled in the centre. Against the wall facing the door was a very large wardrobe, meant for a lady, with compartments at each end for hanging dresses, and rows of drawers of varying sizes filling up the space between.

Woods began to pull open these drawers, carefully avoiding taking hold of the old-fashioned knobs. He achieved his object by inserting the big blade of his pocket-knife into each keyhole in turn, and gradually levering the drawer open sufficiently to enable him to put his hand in and then press each one outwards from within. Most were empty; one or two contained packets of old letters, neatly tied and labelled. Some bundles of photographs and a few books lay in another.

Woods went swiftly through them.

"Seem to be the relics of his marriage," he said briefly to Brown. "These all have to do with his wife."

"If that fellow came in here, he didn't leave much trace," remarked Brown.

"No," returned Woods; "but we know he'd been up here. These papers may be what's left of the more important things. He might have come up here, found what he wanted, and if it were only the size of a packet of letters or what not, he could get off with it in his pockets."

Brown grunted assent. "He wasn't carrying a case or anything. All three who saw him said he'd nothing in his hands, and was fiddling with his collar and hat."

By now Woods had looked through the drawers. He turned towards the hanging cupboards at the end of the wardrobe. There was a key standing in the keyhole at one end, but before touching it Woods threw the beam of his powerful torch on it. What he saw caused him to pause. He made no further effort to open the door, but dispatched Brown to see what the gang of workers below were doing.

While awaiting his return the inspector began to examine the floor with great attention. He had thought on his preliminary hurried visit of investigation that he had detected some small white object lying under the large polished dressing-table. He now began to search more carefully.

As Brown re-entered the room Woods stooped to retrieve the tiny object which he had located lying behind one leg of the dressing-table, and holding it on his palm and centring the bright light of the torch on it, said:

"See here—this is a wax vesta. Under the dressing-table. A freshly struck one. Not an ordinary household match. Mr. Ewing wasn't a smoker, from what I've seen in the other rooms. All the matchboxes there are ordinary safety matches. And what should this fresh match be doing here in an empty, unused room, do you suppose?"

"Lit these candles, I'd say," replied Brown, pointing to two tall, faded, green wax candles which stood in glass sticks on the mantelpiece, relics forgotten and left up here long since.

"Why should he do that? The light's all right," with a glance up towards the lamp overhead. Then, looking at the blinds which were drawn down: "Now, that's an idea; I wonder if the maids who attend to this flat did that? It's run from the hotel, I understand."

He scribbled in his notebook.

"If not, you see, Brown, the murderer pulled them down when he came in here. May not have wanted to turn on the light before he'd got them down. He'd use a match to see his way. Then, perhaps, seeing these candles, he'd just touch them up with his match and make them serve his purpose instead of turning on the light. He'd not be anxious for anyone to see this room too brightly lit up. Candles don't give half the glare of electric light. Well, we've got to see why he came in here at all. This isn't a room that's in use, and we've seen no signs yet of anything valuable up here."

"Perhaps he came in here to hide?" suggested Brown. "He'd hear the nurse and Mr. Godfrey talking outside the flat door. He may have nipped up the stairs, seen the other was the nurse's room, and risked hopping in here. Then thought, after all, he'd better not wait for them to find the body, and made his dash for the stairs and away."

Woods shook his head.

"That doesn't altogether account for the match and the candles. We'll need to look carefully here. The room's been kept pretty clean, but like all unused places there's a certain amount of dust. It's not possible to be sure, but I think the carpet shows there have been people in here lately, more than one set of footmarks, I'd say. It seems to me it's just on the cards Mr. Ewing kept some of his more important papers up here. I've seen no signs of a safe downstairs, nor any deed-boxes or anything of that sort. Old people generally have receptacles where they store away family papers and so on. It's possible too that, like many people who live alone, he used this empty room to keep valuable things in. Old people won't keep things at their banks, and they often think that using a box-room will baffle the petty sneak-thief. This Mr. Ewing too was a cripple. He couldn't get to his bank himself. He'd a wonderful collection here, you know. I suspect he did use this room, for there's no sign of a safe downstairs. This murderer may have known or guessed there was something in here. Anyway, we've got to find out why he came upstairs into this particular room and struck a light."

As he spoke he was examining, without touching, the shabby, faded candles which stood on the mantelpiece.

"Yes, you see, these have both of them been lit recently. The freshly melted wax at the top is a different colour. Burnt for five or six minutes, I'd say. Well, now, let's have a look inside the wardrobe before we do anything else."

Again he was interrupted, this time by the photographer, who came to report they had finished their task below.

"Extraordinary how little disturbance there's been," the man remarked. "Nothing out of the ordinary at all about the room, no upset of any kind."

"No," replied Woods; "the murderer was interrupted right at the outset, before he'd had time."

"Pity it wasn't a bit sooner," murmured the photographer, conscious of the shots he had taken of the body. "Well, we've done, sir; a fresh man is coming on to do anything you want up here. We'll be off. Good night, and good luck."

Chapter VI

THE DETECTIVE

What was once seen, grows what is now described.

The Ring and the Book, R. BROWNING.

Half an hour later, Woods and Riley sat facing each other across a temporary table, set up in the empty box-room. Woods did not want to quit the premises as yet, but so far the body had not been removed. There being no relations, indeed no other occupants of the flat, to be considered, he had decided to leave everything as it had been found for another half-hour or so, until he had completed his preliminary investigation.

Leaving the drawing-room, with its dead owner still lying where he had fallen, and with a man on guard at the door, Woods had, therefore, retreated upstairs. Riley had returned from the station, whence the circular had now been sent out. Brown, having helped Woods in the meticulous search of the drawing-room, had now joined the conference.

"Well," remarked Riley, gazing at what now lay on the table before them, "that's one thing cleared up—Motive. This fellow knew this stuff was here, and that's what he came for. Knew better than to touch the jade and so on. That wasn't marketable—this is."

Woods nodded. Almost idly, his fingers played with the veritable heap of jewellery. Pearl necklaces, diamond bracelets, brooches, rings, all lay scattered before him in profusion. A perfect castle of empty cases was built up at one end of the table. They had formed the contents of the tin box.

"Yes. Now let's just think about this a bit more. Of course a large amount of jewellery like this must have been insured. There'll be a detailed list, probably, at the bank. Riley, you're something of an expert; give me a rough estimate, to be going on with, of what you think this is worth."

Riley glanced at the shining heap, picked up a string of pearls and laid it down again. "Well, of course you know I can only give you a rough idea, but I'd say, myself, between £10,000 and £12,000. It rather depends on the value put on a few special items, like these pearls here."

Woods nodded. "A good figure too, even if the thief only cleared 10 per cent of the value. Now, you two, just listen here a moment. I think the thief was after these things. He hadn't gone for the jade, valuable as that is. None of the cabinets had been unlocked, no fingerprints on the keys or doors, except what are probably Mr. Ewing's—for they're all over the flat. This jewellery was in the tin box in the drawing-room, but the box was down on the floor in the corner by the fireplace, and some of that brown paper and the pieces from the waste-paper basket had slipped and covered it up.

"Actually, the body fell very near the hearth, and some of the blood had spattered out on to the brown paper. I think that accounts for the murderer not lifting it up. He clearly didn't suspect there was anything behind the waste-paper basket, and perhaps didn't want to risk staining his fingers. I think, too, it's pretty clear he never waited to search the drawing-room. He was interrupted before he could do so. He returned up here. Possibly to hide, as Riley suggests. But I think he'd been up here already, before that. The burnt candles suggest that to me. I think he knew Mr. Ewing had valuables in here. For one thing"—nodding to a small tallboy which stood to the left of the empty fireplace behind him—"all the private papers dealing with the collection are there. And see here!" Rising, he went, followed by the two officers, over to the old-fashioned wardrobe. He threw the beam of a torch on the polished wood by the keyhole. Faint smudges and smears, and a few fingerprints showed up in the beam.

"That wardrobe has been opened very recently. Those marks are fresh. Haddon tells me he is pretty sure the fingerprints are Mr. Ewing's. The smudges, of course, are the marks of someone wearing gloves. Now look here!" Taking the edge of the wardrobe door in his fingers, he swung it open, and threw the light of the torch within. On the dull, stained floor of the interior there was a fairly clearly defined patch.

"That's where this tin box has stood. I've measured it up, and the details correspond. I think that box has been kept in here, and, quite recently, Mr. Ewing came and took it out, and removed it to the other room.

"We must try to discover, of course, why that was done. But it's pretty clear to me that the murderer's knowledge told him the box was usually kept here, and this is where he expected to find it. He'd made no great search in Mr. Ewing's bedroom. There were no signs of anything having been disturbed there. He had come in here. That match and those candles show that. There are no wax vestas anywhere else in the house. So we're this much farther on: the murderer knew the house, and he knew about the tin box and its contents. We've got to get on to every man connected or acquainted with Mr. Ewing— every man who might be familiar with the flat, and who answers at all to the description we've got. We've got to find out where every one was, and then perhaps we'll see our way clearer."

"One thing, sir," interrupted Riley, "which joins up with what you're saying. How did the man get in? If he was someone known to Mr. Ewing, of course he'd let him in without suspecting anything, I suppose?"

"We can't be dead sure of that, Riley, yet," replied his superior officer. "He may have had access to the flat as a cleaner or a workman, and had the opportunity to make false keys. This flat is a 'service' flat, you know, with a restaurant attached, and the cleaning of the rooms, bringing up of coal, cleaning of windows, is all done from the central block."

"If that is so," put in Brown, "and the old gentleman went down to his meals, why didn't the murderer wait till he was at dinner? These chaps don't usually kill if they can avoid it."

"Well, Mr. Ewing very often didn't go down to his meals. I've talked to the proprietress of the flats. She tells me he liked to get down to the restaurant when he could, but if his arthritis was bad he'd have his meals up here. She says he'd been better lately, but she doesn't remember if he'd been down yesterday. The nurse will know, but I can't see her yet. And, in any case, the proprietress says she believes he never left the flat empty for long. He'd come down to the restaurant with the nurse, but when she'd seen him to his table she'd come back up here. The flat would only be left while she was taking or fetching him from the restaurant, and not for more than five minutes at a time."

"Why did he do that, sir?" queried Riley.

"Well, as far as I can make out, this collection of jade is a good one. It's very valuable in itself, and the individual pieces, some of them, are worth a lot. It's portable too, and a thief getting in could make a good haul if he were in touch with the right people. That's another point—the collection was quite well known to a lot of people. Now the murderer didn't go for the jade. It seems probable, to put it at the lowest, that he was after this jewellery in the tin box. We've got to find out about the jewellery, of course, but it looks to me as if it had been the property of the late Mrs. Ewing. That being so, it wouldn't be used, nor, most likely, looked at. That box probably stayed in here for months on end without being opened." He paused, and glanced interrogatively at his companions. Both nodded their agreement, and he continued: "If that were so, the thief, if he came just to rob, might reckon he'd get away quietly with the box, and the theft not be noticed for a while. Jade taken from the shelves would, of course, leave gaps which would be noticed straight away."

"That's an indication that he meant to rob, but not murder," put in Riley. "He may have thought he'd get in here, and away, without being heard."

Woods nodded. "Yes, it's possible. But, of course, when he came up here to-night the box wasn't in its place."

Then, turning to the sergeant: "Well, Riley, you'd better start checking up all the hotel staff, I think. Find where this stuff is insured, and get an inventory and so on."

"H'm! Plenty of routine work for me," said Riley grimly. "Well, sir, I'll be off, and start. There'll be a night staff on now round at the hotel. They come in at 8.30, I'm told, and I'll take the opportunity of going through there straight away." He glanced at the clock, which marked nearly 9 o'clock. Woods experienced a faint sensation of surprise. Less than four hours had passed since the discovery of the crime, and yet so much had been fitted in. He had the familiar sensation which often accompanied his investigations, as if he had picked up a roll, which, slowly unfolding before him, gradually brought into view the lives, the habits, the personalities of people who, only a brief while before, had been totally unknown to him. Already he had a conception of the life lived by the dead man, of his tastes, his wealth, his way of life. Now he desired to unroll the scroll still farther, and obtain a knowledge of his friends, his associates, and the various people, of all ranks of life, who had, in the past, entered the flat.

Anne Godfrey, in the flat below, was conscious of something of the same sort, as she sat, vainly trying to compose her distracted mind by tidying up her room.

Poor Nurse Edwards had gone to some relations, for the doctor had judged that it would give her nerves a better chance of recovery if she moved right away from the neighbourhood of the crime. Anne was busily putting away sal-volatile, rolling up bandages, replacing pots of boracic ointment, restoring her aunt's well-stocked medicine cupboard to its usual neatness, but all the while her brain ceaselessly reverted to Henry, who, with his wife, had now gone off to their own home.

The tension of his nerves had given way to violent irritability once the police had been and gone. Doreen's inane exclamations and repetitions, and Mrs. Dutton's ceaseless lamentations, had maddened him beyond bearing, and, after one furious outburst, which reduced them all to silence, he had bidden Doreen get her things on, and they had taken their departure. Peace had descended once more on the flat. Mrs. Dutton had gone to bed, and Anne had set herself to efface the signs of Nurse Edwards's presence. She, and Inspector Woods in the next flat, and Henry himself in his own home, were now all really thinking along the same lines.

"*Poor* Henry," thought Anne. "I can't help being sorry for him. If *only* he'd stopped that man. If *only* he'd even shut the door behind him. Or if he had only had a better view of his face! I'm afraid everyone will be down on him, and think—and say—he behaved like a fool!"

She sighed, for she knew Henry had enough to embitter his temper as it was, and she envisaged a marked increase in its violence in the course of the next few weeks. "Doreen will only make this worse too," she reflected. "Why on earth did he ever marry her! Life's going to be more difficult for them both than ever. In fact we're all of us in for a bad time," she thought. With a very shadowed face, she finished putting the room to rights.

"Curse it all!" ran Henry's meditations. "Now I'm in for the devil of a lot of unpleasantness! Everyone'll call me a fool or a coward! 'What! You *saw* the man, and didn't stop him? Didn't ask him his business? Was he a very formidable sort of person?' Oh! devil take it all! What a damned beastly affair!" and maddened by the endless questioning, police, press and lawyers, which he saw stretching ahead of him for days and even weeks, he jumped up and began restlessly pacing up and down, until his wife, her nerves badly shaken by the events of the evening, took refuge in early bed, leaving him to the gloom of his own thoughts.

Woods, pondering over the case as he sat making up his notes in the spare-room of Ewing's flat, also considered the conduct of Henry, though from rather a different angle.

"Mr. Godfrey"—he looked at the name heading a page in his notebook—"ought to be a good witness. He's cool enough, and steady enough, I'm sure. Lucky he was on the spot; he ought to be able to help us to fix up times." For Woods had already decided that an exact time-table was going to be a very important feature of the case.

"Now, let's see. His wife had been at Mrs. Dutton's flat since 3 o'clock. Neither she, nor Mrs. Dutton, nor Miss Godfrey noticed any noise or anything above. Mr. Godfrey came in to tea before 5 o'clock. They all agree it was within ten minutes of the hour. Heard the fall approximately 5.15. Nurse Edwards came in at about 5.25. She and Mr. Godfrey went up—5.25–30. Saw the man in the flat then.

"Now, Nurse Edwards had been out since 4 o'clock. Mr. Ewing had been alone since then, as far as is known. Murder definitely took place between 4 and 5.30, probably at 5.15. That crash *must* have been the body, I suppose?"

Up to the present, the flat had remained exactly as it had been when the police first entered. Search had been made for a possible weapon, but everything had been left, as far as possible, in its original position.

Again Woods visualized the room. It had shown no signs whatever of disorder; nothing had fallen over; nothing had been broken, no door or cupboard had been smashed open.

He rose and went down to the room below, still guarded by the man on duty in the flat itself. He decided to go over, for one final time before sending for the ambulance, the exact state of affairs in the drawing-room. He felt that personalities must wait. He must get the details of the scene imprinted on his mind while everything was fresh.

The body still lay where it had been found, awaiting his instructions for its removal. Mr. Ewing had, he surmised, been seated in his arm-chair, presumably tidying up after dispatching letters or parcels. Woods noted the scraps of brown paper, ends of string, pieces of sealing-wax. He observed that ordinary Bryant and May's matches of the large size had been used, and the burnt-out ends had been neatly laid in a pen tray.

A chair had been pushed to one side, one of rather a beautiful set, solid, heavy Chippendale. The body lay on the ground, so close to it that the legs were spattered with blood. He observed that the chair had been turned round, so that the back legs were nearest the corpse.

Clearly the murderer had done his work either kneeling, or standing by the body, in the place where his victim had first fallen. Blood had spurted towards the fireplace, on to the fire-irons, some on to the coal scuttle. But there was none towards the table, none anywhere else at all. Pools had soaked in round the head, but otherwise the room was extraordinarily free from any signs of disturbance. Woods felt it was almost uncanny. With the body out of sight behind the table, anyone coming in would see only a beautiful, peaceful room, gay with flowers, well lit, well warmed. Yet once step round that table, catch but one glimpse of what lay on the floor, and that peaceful room surpassed in horror any shambles or place of execution.

Struck afresh by the concentration of the area where blood was to be found, Woods bent down to scrutinize the rug. Turning to his notes, he saw that Godfrey and the nurse had found the body covered up. The rug lay, where Woods himself had thrown it, across an arm-chair.

It was a silk Persian rug, of beautiful design and texture—the main colouring being a deep rose red.

Picking it up, Woods found it was deeply stained on both sides. He could not decide whether this was due to the blood having actually soaked right through. Considering the fact that the rug was thick and close, and that it could not have lain over the body for any very great length of time, he decided that this was a point which must be looked into.

He noted that the hands of the corpse were uninjured. As Dr. Carr had said, the victim had apparently offered no resistance. Probably he had been stunned by the first blow. There were no rings on his fingers, but, peering very closely, Woods thought he could perceive on the left hand a sort of callus or indentation, as if a ring or rings had been habitually worn and had marked the finger. Noting that this point must be verified by the doctor, and having now satisfied himself that he had let no detail of what was actually presented to his eyes escape him, he at length gave the order for the ambulance men to be notified and for the body to be removed to the mortuary.

It was getting late, but, before going off duty for the night, he felt there was one more task to be done. He wanted to obtain some light on the possible ways in which the murderer might have entered the flat.

He discovered two things almost at once. The front door of the flat itself was opened by a Yale lock of the ordinary pattern. There were bolts as well and a chain, but, clearly, as in most flats, the door was usually opened by the Yale lock. The catch was set back, so that the door could be opened by the simple insertion of the key; the safety catch was pressed back out of action.

Going down the staircase to the main exit to the street, Woods examined the front door there. This was a new one, put in when the house was converted, and made to match the Duttons' door, which adjoined. Both doors were solid, new, and the paint in good condition.

The lock, again, was Yale, with the catch set back. It had not been forced, or tampered with. Inquiries from the porter at the hotel, and from Mrs. Dutton, had elicited the fact that this lower door was left open during the day, and only closed at night. Thus, anyone visiting Mr. Ewing's flat could go in from the street, mount the stairs, and there be unperceived and unheard from the street, while, as the flatlets above were both empty, there would be no interruption from that quarter. Once Mr. Ewing were left alone, with the nurse out, anyone would have had ample time and opportunity to get into the flat. Assuming, too, that the old man were suffering from his arthritis, it might be anticipated that he would be more or less stationary in his room, he would not be likely to have been moving about the flat itself.

Woods realized that for the present he had done all that could be done. Further details must wait until the morning, when it was to be hoped Nurse Edwards would be sufficiently recovered to give him accurate information on the many points where he felt she could enlighten him.

He had very little hope that the circular, now issued to the police, would bring in any information as to the fugitive, and with the conviction that the probable solution as to his identity lay in the circumstances and staging of the murder itself, rather than in any possible identification from outside, he turned his face thankfully away from No. 5B Clevedon Street. When next he had occasion to visit that flat, at least it would no longer contain the grim presence, formerly Simon Ewing.

Chapter VII

THE DEALER

Later or sooner by a minute then.

The Ring and the Book, R. BROWNING.

The next morning dawned bright, clear and cold. The rain had stopped, the sun was shining, the street looked fresh and clean in the palely brilliant December light. London sparkled and rejoiced, and all the shops, bright with Christmas goods, radiated gaiety.

There was no gaiety at No. 5 Clevedon Street. Mrs. Dutton, thoroughly shaken by the murder, was beginning to wonder whether she would shut up the flat at once, and go elsewhere until the excitement and notoriety caused by the crime had subsided. Two considerations deterred her. First, the prosaic fact that she had wakened up with all the symptoms of a heavy cold, caught probably in the draughts of the preceding night. She was at present in bed, and Dr. Ainslie had told her quite firmly that she must remain there for a day or two at least, perhaps longer.

The second factor was Anne's strongly expressed wish to make no move. Anne had spent a sleepless night, and two things had become clear to her. She herself must be a prominent witness, owing to the encounter with the man in the porch, and the police would certainly require her to be at hand, in case of any possible identification. She could not hope to carry out her plans, and go off to the south of France, at any rate for several weeks. She was also pretty confident that her brother and his wife would need her. Henry had a great deal of anxiety to contend with in his business, for the slump had hit him hard, and Anne knew that he was nervous with regard to his financial affairs. She also realized that he too would be involved in the trial. Bitterly she regretted that she had let him go up, the night before, with Nurse Edwards. It had been on the tip of her tongue to offer to go up herself. She told herself that she had held back simply because Henry had so "let himself go" in speaking to their aunt. She had been ashamed of his display of temper and lack of self-control, and she had thought to herself that he could go up with Nurse Edwards as a sort of reparation. Vaguely, she had been rather shocked by his irritability, and had felt that he needed a lesson. Now she whole-heartedly regretted the episode. Henry was clearly in no state to bear the extra worry, tension, and loss of time involved in a murder case. Anne resolved that she, in her turn, would try to atone for what she now felt to have been her own self-righteousness. She would stay in town, do her best to help Doreen to ease the situation, and, as far as she could, help Henry himself.

So she had got up with the decision to try and persuade her aunt to let her, at least, stay on in the flat, and had secretly been much relieved to find that for the present at any rate they must both remain.

Telephoning to her brother's house, she heard from Doreen that Henry had already gone to work, and Doreen, thoroughly unsettled and uneasy alone by herself, had eagerly responded to Anne's suggestion that she should come round to the flat and talk things over.

Now the two were sitting, silent for a moment, by the fireside, having already discussed the unfortunate effect the whole business was likely to have on Henry.

Doreen had reported him as plunged in gloom, refusing to talk at breakfast, and merely resenting any efforts on the part of his wife to cheer him up.

Now, both were reflecting how hard it was that perfectly ordinary people, going about their lawful occasions, should find themselves involved in so shattering a business as a murder. Inevitably they had less sympathy to spare for the victim, whom both had known, and whom both had disliked, than for Henry himself, who seemed doomed to go through a great deal of unpleasantness. Yet, Anne thought to herself, she, in the same circumstances, would probably have behaved in exactly the same way. Fear of making a mistake, of putting oneself in a ridiculous light, of making an unnecessary fuss in some other person's house, all these were motives which would have caused most people to pause and do nothing, only to realize too late that, for once, violent and instant action had been required.

With a start, Anne was brought back to reality by the sound of an electric bell shrilling faintly from above.

"Oh, Doreen!" she exclaimed, jumping to her feet in excitement— and then she and her sister-in-law both stood staring at one another. "It's Mr. Ewing's bell," Anne went on, after a moment. "Someone has gone up to his flat who hasn't heard the news. It's not in the papers yet, you know!"

"Well, the police are up there," replied her sister-in-law. "They'll answer the door."

But Anne was looking at her with an intentness which caused Doreen in her turn to pause.

"Doreen, you know, when that bell sounded like that, it reminded me of something. Didn't it ring last night? Some time or other when you were here? But before we heard that fall?"

Doreen grew pale at the very recollection of the crash which had been, for them, the signal of so much. Instinctively she glanced up at the ceiling. Then, with a clearer memory returning to her of the events of the preceding night, she said: "Yes, I think you're right. I'm almost sure the bell did ring. You know, you can only hear it in here if their downstairs door is open, and if ours is open too."

Anne's face lit up with a gleam. "That was why we heard it last night. I was in my room, and came out to let Henry in when I heard him coming up the steps. He was standing blocking up the way, pulling his coat off in the hall, and I hadn't got past him to shut the door. I could hear that bell ringing in Mr. Ewing's flat quite fairly clearly."

Doreen hesitated for a moment. Then: "Do you think it's important? Shall you have to tell the police that?"

"Why, yes; I think we must. You see, it may be *very* important. It means that someone rang, and Mr. Ewing must have let them in, for he was alone then, you know; Nurse Edwards was out."

Hardly had the words crossed her lips, than she realized their full meaning." Oh, Doreen! If it was somebody he allowed in, don't you think it must have been somebody he knew?"

Doreen looked at her in silence for a moment. Then: "It might simply have been a tradesman delivering a parcel late. But—" She stopped, and then, with rising excitement, and obviously unable to refrain from giving expression to the thought which had come into her head, she gave a quick glance round to see if the door was shut, and then added: "Oh, Anne! I wonder if George Fordham has a good alibi!"

Anne looked at her sister-in-law in astonishment, then spoke rather coldly: "I don't, of course, know George Fordham, though I've heard you and Henry speak of him and Penelope, but I'm sure you oughtn't to be talking like that of him."

"Oh, don't be tiresome, Anne!" retorted her sister-in-law. "I didn't say I accused him! I simply mean he's a horrible young man with a very poor sort of reputation, and, of course, he's going to gain a great deal from his uncle's death. He's a person with a motive, and he's also someone Mr. Ewing would have let into the house, even if he were alone in it!"

"Those are flimsy grounds on which to suspect anyone," said Anne stiffly. "You can't really *know* whether he will benefit from his uncle's death. The money may all go to someone else."

"Oh no!" answered Doreen eagerly. "I've often heard him grumbling and swearing, and saying that he knew his old uncle had left him 'the cash', but that he wouldn't on any account help him with a bean in his lifetime."

"Well," said Anne, turning away impatiently, "I don't think you ought to be fitting a halter round anyone's neck like that. You ought to hold your tongue, if it's only for the sake of his wife, to whom you say you're so devoted."

"Oh!" retorted Doreen, made reckless by Anne's disapproval, and instigated thereby to justify herself. "If it weren't for the scandal, I should say it would be a good thing for Penelope if George *were* out of the way. He really is a beast, and she must go through hell with him. She won't leave him, though we've all begged and urged her to do so, and I'd just think myself anything was a blessing which rid her of him!"

Realizing that she had gone rather far, she stopped; but Anne, in disgust, had walked away, and now went out of the room, leaving her sister-in-law to reflect that once more she had forgotten how bitterly Anne hated gossip, and how strictly she expected her friends to bridle the tongue, that "unruly member".

Meanwhile, Henry, full of anger and apprehension, had gone, not, as his wife believed, to his office, but in answer to a summons to Inspector Woods's room at the police station, and, girding himself up to meet the ordeal which he knew lay before him, went up the steps of the station as the clock struck ten, and was shown at once into the private office.

There Woods greeted him, and, begging him to sit down, at once prepared to question him. For a night's interval had convinced

Woods that there still existed some hope that Godfrey might be able to help him in certain particulars. The nurse, he was sure, from all he had heard, would not be very likely to give him reliable and detailed accounts of the matters he was most anxious to investigate. She had been confused and agitated by her accident before ever she went up to the flat, and was still rather inclined to be hysterical. Woods had early perceived that certain facts might act as lamps, lighting up stretches of the darkness surrounding the crime, and perhaps in the end throwing a beam on the figure of the murderer at present lost in the shadows. He had already, in accordance with his practice, tabulated the points he wished to establish, in this order:

I.   *The jewels.* If these were to be considered as having a bearing on the crime, it was essential to find out certain details.

    (a) Who knew of their existence? Did the members of the family? Did the nurse? Did the neighbours?

    (b) What were they worth? Were they insured, and if so who had valued them?

    (c) Had they been the property of Mr. Ewing, absolutely, or were they held by him in trust as heirlooms?

II.   *What men* were in the habit of visiting the flat?

    (a) Friends of Simon Ewing.

    (b) Members of his family.

    (c) Friends of the nurse.

    (d) Persons employed by the flats.

III. *What was the exact sequence of events* connected with the crime?

    (a) Was the nurse known to be out?

    (b) When had she fetched help?

    (c) At what time had the crash been heard?

    (d) What interval elapsed before she and Godfrey entered
        the flat?

He began, therefore, by inquiring from Henry whether Mr. Ewing was known to be wealthy?

Henry replied that he had always understood Mr. Ewing had a large income, and had concluded, from the fact that he was quite a well-known collector of jade, that he had a good deal of capital expended on his collection.

Woods then put to him the question:

"Did you know, Mr. Godfrey, that besides his jade and crystal Mr. Ewing had a considerable amount of very valuable jewellery in his flat?"

Henry stared in amaze. He had been fortifying himself to meet questions as to the man he had seen, and to be thoroughly cross-examined over that man's actions and appearance. He was unprepared for this inquiry and, surly and suspicious, he answered no. He had never bothered about Mr. Ewing's affairs, nor heard much about them. He had never heard anyone mention any jewellery.

Pressed by the inspector, he added, rather spitefully: "Well, I know my wife never said a thing about any jewellery, and she was very thick with George Fordham's wife. I'd have expected to have heard a lot if there'd been any talk."

"Ah, yes!" said Woods thoughtfully. "Mr. George Fordham, of course, is the nephew and next-of-kin. I'm expecting him along here this morning. Well, then, Mr. Godfrey, I'm to take it that neither you nor your wife knew of this hoard of jewellery upstairs?"

"That's correct, Inspector," replied Henry.

"And as you yourself are an expert in precious stones, Mr. Godfrey, I suppose you'd have been all the more likely to have recollected if such a matter had ever been mentioned before you?"

Henry laughed, rather sourly. "I see you've been looking us all up, Inspector. Gone into our records, and all that, already. Well, I suppose it's what I've got to expect now!" With a sudden outburst of impotent rage, he added: "If that cursed old man hadn't kept all that stuff there, I suppose none of this would ever have happened." And, with a gesture of violent disgust, he buried his head in his hands.

The inspector remained silent, gazing at him rather curiously, till Henry, lifting his haggard face, said: "Sorry, Inspector, I ought not to have spoken like that, but this is going to be a beastly affair for me, you know! And I've enough worries of my own, with this slump looking as if it would never end!"

"Yes, sir," said Woods, non-committally, and, in a practical, matter-of-fact voice, he added: "I think the best thing we can do now is for you to answer my questions, and get that part over. Now, sir," resuming his official manner, "the next point I want you to help me with is this. Can you tell me at all what men were familiar with Mr. Ewing's flat, and who, so far as you know, were the men most likely to visit him?"

Henry shook his head. "I can't help you there, Inspector. Actually, I don't often go to my aunt's flat. My wife is more of a visitor there than I am."

"Did you know Mr. Ewing yourself, sir?"

"Yes, but only very slightly. I knew his nephew quite well, and he took me up there once to see the collection. That's the only time I ever saw the old gentleman."

"Do you know of anyone else who visited him?"

"No, I don't," said Henry impatiently. "My aunt is more likely to tell you all that. She was his neighbour. I wasn't. It's wasting time to ask me."

"Well, I just thought, as it is men friends or acquaintances I'm after, you might have known something useful," said Woods apologetically. "And I've got to go dredging about everywhere, you know."

Then, making up his mind to come to rather closer quarters: "I'll come, then, Mr. Godfrey, to something you *can* tell me about! I want you to describe to me what you yourself heard and saw and did last night. Tell it me in your own words, and I'll ask you to explain anything that strikes me as specially important."

Realizing that from this there could be no escape, Godfrey braced himself wearily, and began. He gave a brief, clear account of the tea-party at his aunt's flat, and of the noise they had all heard while they were waiting for tea.

"Now, sir," interrupted Woods, "this is very important, and I want you to go carefully. Tell me every detail you can recollect. First, what time was it when you arrived at your aunt's house?"

Henry paused and thought. "I had meant to be there at 4.30, and was expected then, but I was detained, and I wasn't punctual. I think I got there some time before five, say between ten and five minutes to the hour, not later."

"And when did you hear the noise?"

"We were waiting for the kettle to boil. The crash came before tea was made. I remember the kettle boiled over while we were all silent, listening. I looked round at my aunt and up at the clock, and it said just past five—not quite five past. I think that would be so, you know, for the kettle was put on directly I went in, and it had been standing in the hearth and was fairly hot, so that it wouldn't take more than a few minutes to bring it to the boil."

Henry's nervousness tended to make him voluble, thought Woods, as he made a careful note.

"Then just tell me, as clearly as you can, what happened next."

Henry paused, and went on slowly:" We all talked for a bit, and then Nurse Edwards rang at the door. That would be about 5.20 or 5.25. She came in, and explained to us she'd not been able to open the door of Mr. Ewing's flat, and wanted one of us to go up. She told us she'd rung two or three times." He broke off, staring at the inspector." If that was so—if that was so—why, she must have stood there ringing while he was murdering the old man inside!

Woods looked up. "Yes, that is so," he said concisely. I've Riley's report of Nurse Edwards's statement. She says she rang two or three times. No one answered, but she heard someone moving in the flat, and concluded Mr. Ewing deliberately didn't want to answer the door." He stopped, and for a moment both men sat silent.

Before the mind of each was a picture of that little scene. Each visualized the lovely drawing-room, with a prostrate figure, and, kneeling by that body, a man, striking and striking, while, only a few yards away, separated by nothing more than a glass-panelled door, the woman had stood quietly waiting for that bell to be answered.

Woods's mind flashed back to the body, as he had seen it. Probably the nurse's action had been even more fatal than she realized. The murderer had already knocked down his victim. That was known from the time fixed by the Duttons' tea. But he might not have meant to kill. Often men, intending to commit robbery with violence, would knock down and stun their victim, and then go off to make sure of their booty. But this robber had been interrupted by that bell. Its shrill clangour had told him that someone was standing at the door—some-one who, in all probability, as the bell rang again, was anxious to get in—and who might possibly force an entrance or fetch help to do so. In a frenzied determination to silence his victim, to prevent his call-ing out and bringing that person outside bursting in to the rescue, he had struck again and again. Or, perhaps, merely driven frantic with terror by the belief that he was about to be caught red-handed, he had been filled with a mad resolve to make certain, to finish the work he had begun, and so those innumerable blows had rained down on that unprotected head and face, making speech or cry, or even sound, impossible for ever.

With an inward shudder, Woods switched his mind away from those thoughts. He began to speak again, his voice hard and metallic.

"So you and the nurse went up together?"

"Yes, I went with her, and my sister, as it happens, followed us, though that I didn't know at the moment."

" Time?"

"Just before 5.30, I should say."

"Did you talk at all as you went up?"

"Yes, a little—not much, but I did say a word or two about her accident."

"Do you think your voices would sound up the staircase?"

" I suppose mine would. The nurse was feeling rather shaken. She spoke in rather a low voice. We talked a little as we stood at the door before I got it open, that I am sure of. We were a little delayed by her having only her left arm to fumble in her bag for the key. I had to take her bag in the end. I know we were talking then."

Woods glanced at his notes. "When you went in, you stood inside the flat?"

"Yes, I stood for a moment on the mat, with my back to the lobby, pulling the key out of the door. Then I stood waiting, in case Mr. Ewing would see me, and to make sure the nurse was all right. She went towards the drawing-room, and at the same time the man came down the small staircase at the end of the passage."

Henry spoke now in a completely colourless, unemotional voice.

"And the man's appearance, as far as you can give it?"

"Fairly tall, about five foot ten or so. Slim. I should say fair, fresh complexioned. A light coloured coat, and a soft hat. He had spectacles—I saw the light catch them."

"H'm," said Woods." Fair, you think? Your sister, you know, thought he was dark."

"Well," retorted Henry, "I thought him fair. But I can't really say. How could I have noticed much? He walked rather quickly towards me. He was putting on his hat and turning up his collar. You can't see much of a man in a moment like that."

"Had he a moustache?"

" I couldn't see—his hand was up, pulling on his hat, and hid the lower part of his face."

"Would you say he was a working man? What sort of impression did he make on you?"

Henry hesitated. "No. I didn't take him for a working man. I thought he was a visitor. Someone staying there for Christmas, or who'd looked in on Mr. Ewing. He didn't shuffle or hurry. Seemed quite at home. That's what kept me quiet till he'd passed. That and the nurse taking no notice of him."

Woods nodded. He couldn't altogether blame Godfrey. Yet, if only he'd stood squarely in the doorway, so that the man would have had to push past or speak! Even that would have been some help, would have given a better idea of the fellow. It was no good, however, and the best had to be made of what had been seen.

"Do you think you could identify him?"

"Not a hope, Inspector. He seemed quite ordinary to me. Lots of fellows like him. Nothing outstanding to go by whatever."

"Well," said Woods, "I'm sorry, of course, Mr. Godfrey, that you can't be more definite. Still, you've helped us a good deal. Just one or two more questions and I've done. Did you notice any stains on this light coat you speak of?"

"No, I didn't!" said Henry strongly. "Of course I didn't! I'm quite sure he had no stains or marks on that coat at all, and he wasn't rumpled or tousled in any way. Nothing at all odd or untidy about him at all. He looked perfectly normal and all right, Inspector, in every way."

"Was he wearing gloves?"

"No," replied Henry, after a moment's thought, "I'm pretty sure he was not. I think I remember his bare hand up at his hat brim."

Woods nodded. In one sense he was glad. He had an idea simmering in his head, which Henry's words confirmed, and, anxious now to return to the flat and verify this, he began pinning his notes together.

"Yes, that would be so, I think, Mr. Godfrey. Well, that will be all now, thank you. Good day."

Then, as Henry, with obvious relief, was turning to go: "Just one moment. I want to get clear about the rug. What did you do with that?"

"I lifted it," said Henry, keeping his face and voice stiff, "and I saw what was underneath, and dropped the rug back."

"Did you pick it right off?"

"Yes, I had to. It was sort of crumpled all round him—almost tucked in, in fact. I couldn't see till I'd got it lifted quite clear."

"And then you—?"

"I flung it down again, and covered him up."

" Did you notice which side you put it down?"

"Oh, good heavens, no! I just threw it down as quickly as I could. I didn't stop to see *how* I did it. I felt"—he paused, then went on—"I felt it was all wet and sticky, and I wanted to let go of it as quickly as I could."

Again Woods nodded comprehension. Again he had got the little piece of confirmation he wanted for the theory which he was building up in his mind.

"Thank you very much, Mr. Godfrey. Now that really is all. I shan't, I think, need to see you again just yet. You'll be notified, of course, of the inquest."

Henry, ruefully aware that the inquest would be more of an ordeal than this interview, went off to his office. Woods, slightly more cheerful than before, prepared to interview the man in whom he was already deeply interested, George Fordham, the murdered man's nephew and heir.

Chapter VIII

THE HEIR

A tale comes to my mind, possibly true, probably false.

Guido, R. BROWNING.

G eorge Fordham came into the inspector's room with an unmistakable air of defiance. He threw his hat and gloves down on
the table, and, in answer to Woods's request that he would sit down,
he flung himself into the chair drawn up at the side of the desk, and
turned his eyes towards Woods with a sort of unfriendly boldness that
at once aroused hostility.

He was a tall, thin, dark young man, with cadaverous cheeks and
a certain raffish air, resembling a tousled hawk.

At the moment, his appearance was not improved by a strip of
plaster which ran from the corner of his mouth up towards his ear,
giving him a somewhat piratical appearance.

Seeing the inspector looking inquisitively at this decoration,
Fordham began at once—in an aggressively flippant tone:

"Sorry I look such a disreputable person, Inspector. All this fuss, and
the liquid support I had to give myself to bear up last night, made my hand
a bit unsteady this morning. Gave myself a baddish cut. Had to get our
local sawbones to patch me up. Yes, he'll tell you all about it"—quickly,
seeing the sceptical look which Woods could not prevent from crossing
his face, though he instantly tried to repress it—"I've not been scrapping
with my wife, or having plates thrown at me. So you needn't look so
disgusted and high-minded. Anyone's at liberty to cut himself, shaving."

Anxious as he was to avoid any preconceived prejudice, the inspector realized that in this man he was going to find no friendliness or co-operation.

Laying his notebook in front of him, he prepared to listen and question. But before he could start:

"Well, Inspector," went on his visitor provocatively, "I suppose this is going to be a miserable affair?"

"It's a very unhappy one, certainly, Mr. Fordham," retorted Woods drily." The murder of an elderly gentleman, and, I gather, your only near relative, is bound to cause you a good deal of trouble."

He paused, for George Fordham burst at once into a loud, harsh laugh.

"Trouble! Well, yes, trouble in one sense, Inspector, but not in another. I'm not going to make any pretences at all. I dare say you'd see through them if I did," he added insolently. "My uncle was no sort of use to me when he was alive. Treated me damned badly. There was no love lost between us, I can tell you. And I'm not going to pretend that I feel any sorrow for his death. I shan't be troubled by his loss in that sense! But I suppose you're going to give me a lot of bother over it all, that I can foresee for myself. I'm going to be a busy man now, too, I can tell you, so let's get on with it. You've a whole pack of questions you want to put me, I imagine."

Seeing that no sympathy or tact need be expended on George Fordham, Woods came at once to the point.

"Very well, Mr. Fordham, I'll be glad of any information you can give me with regard to your uncle's way of life and his associates."

"Precious little I can tell you. He and I didn't hobnob. I don't suppose I set foot in his flat more than once a year. His friends weren't mine, either, I can tell you. He'd an old crony—a Major Anstruther—whom he saw fairly often, I believe. And he saw that doctor fellow opposite pretty regularly. Otherwise he'd no men friends or acquaintances that I know of. I suppose it's men you're after, isn't it?"

The glance which accompanied this remark startled Woods. There was a malevolence, a slyness about it, which cast light on George Fordham's disposition at any rate.

"Yes, sir, you're right. I want to try and account for every man, known to Mr. Ewing, who might have visited his flat, and whom he would readily have admitted."

"H'm, yes. I realized all that," replied Fordham. "I'm no fool, you know, Inspector, whatever else I may be! That nurse being out, the old man would have opened the door himself."

"Might have done so," corrected Woods. "There are other possibilities."

Fordham stared. "Do you mean that the man might have been hidden in the flat before the nurse went out?"

Woods, however, refused to say what was in his mind. "We needn't discuss that now, sir. What I want you to give me, if you can, is a list of Mr. Ewing's friends—as far as you can give me one. Was he, for example, in the habit of having people come to see his collection? Other people interested in it, I mean, collectors, dealers, and so on?"

George shook his head. "No. He was a sour old fellow, and didn't fraternize with other old birds. He was too jealous. Didn't like people to know what he'd got, and didn't want to hear them boast about what *they'd* got."

"But you took people up there to see the jade—so I understand?"

For a moment George looked nonplussed.

"Took people up?"

"Yes. Mr. Godfrey told me you took him up on one occasion."

"Yes, I did. And that was about the one and only time! Godfrey's a friend of mine, so, of course, that was enough to put the old man off. Said he didn't want to be brought into contact with his neighbours either—Godfrey is Mrs. Dutton's nephew, you know. So I never took anyone else."

"What about the people he bought his things from?"

"Don't know anything about that. I know he always dealt with one special firm, who bought for him. I imagine his lawyer, or his banker, knows. I didn't really take any interest myself in the collection or anything to do with it. A damned waste of money, I always thought it!"

"Well," said Woods patiently, "then you really can't tell me anything more on that point?"

A defiant nod from George.

"Then, sir, we come to the next point. You realize, of course, I must ask you where you yourself were, yesterday evening, between the hours of four and six? A matter of routine we must go through."

Fordham grinned maliciously. "Shall it be a too perfect alibi, Inspector, or will you do without one?"

Woods making no answer to this sally, he went on: "Well, I haven't got an alibi at all. I was at my office—141B Great Queen Street—until a quarter-past five o'clock. Then, as usual, I came home, travelling by tube. It was, as you know, the rush hour. I didn't see anyone I knew on my way back. I got home at about 5.45. I didn't go into my own flat, for I met the man from the next door flat as I was going up the stairs—we don't rise to a lift in our buildings. He asked me to go in and have a smoke and a drink, so I did. I stayed in there talking to him, and so I never heard the telephone going in our own flat. My wife had been rung up from the Dutton's, and she had heard all about the murder, but she didn't know I was in next door, and didn't know how to get hold of me. I went back in to our place about seven, expecting a meal then. Didn't get one though. She was all done in by the news of the affair, and in the end I had to take her out and get a meal at the nearest place before I went off to my uncle's flat."

"This friend can, of course, corroborate your story?"

"Of course." Again that insolent grin.

"Had your wife been in all the evening?"

"As far as I know. She was there, anyway, when Henry Godfrey rang up at about half-past six. She answered the phone, and says he didn't want to tell her, at first, what was wrong. She got the wind up—she knew from the way he spoke there was something up—and thought it might have been an accident to me, as I wasn't back. So he had to tell her. She was in a frightful state about it. Tender-hearted, you know. More so than I am!"

He stopped, and surveyed Woods with a truculent air.

"Who have you at your office?" inquired Woods, calmly. "Have you anyone who can confirm your statement that you left at five o'clock?"

"No, no one. I'm a free-lance, inspector—work on my own. I've an agency for a floor-covering, and I get an office and my expenses out of it—precious little else. I don't run to a staff—or even an office boy."

"Is there a porter, or commissionaire, at your office buildings?"

"Oh yes; there's a fellow who works the lift, but he wasn't about— often isn't—and I worked it myself."

A brief silence. Fordham's expression hardened. "You know as well as I do, Inspector, a man can't prove his whereabouts at a moment's notice. I'll inquire amongst my friends, and see if any of them noticed me on my way home. But I didn't notice them, and I don't suppose I'll have any luck. I've had rotten luck all my life," he went on, with a spurt of resentment, "and it's going to stay rotten, I should say. My old uncle dies, and I hope I'm going to be comfortably provided for, but of course that's to be complicated by an alibi, and the hell of a lot of trouble."

"I'm sorry, of course, sir," said Woods, more stiffly than ever; "but at the same time, I clearly must ask you to obtain corroboration of your statement. As to any progress we make in our investigation, of course you'll be kept informed."

Fordham, who, if he regretted the bad impression he had obviously made, showed no signs of repentance, rose to go, with a very lowering face.

"Well, I'll do what I can, but it's for you, you know, to make a case, not for me to disprove it!" and with that last glint of bravado he went.

Woods spoke down the telephone. "That you, Curtis? Set on foot inquiries into Mr. George Fordham's occupation. He tells me he's an agent for floorcloth. Address, 141B Great Queen Street. Find out everything you can about his finances, and about his friends, and, of course, anything about his movements yesterday. Right."

Putting down the receiver, he meditated a moment. He had been definitely antagonized by Fordham. "That man's a wrong un," he thought to himself. "Heartless as they're made; not a word of pity for that poor old uncle, not a mention of the circumstances. Sneering at his wife for showing a little feeling. Only thinking of himself, and any possible disadvantages to his position. I don't like him. And we'll keep a strict eye upon him. Wonder what sort of a wife he's got?"

With the reflection that she too might be interviewed, and realizing he had a heavy day before him, Woods dismissed his musings, and turned to the first name on his list.

"'Beatrice Edwards.' Well, now, she ought to be important. She might have something to tell if she's calmed down at all by now." And eager to obtain any glimpses of light that might be shed on the events of the preceding night, he put on his hat and, going out of the station, bade the police car, which was waiting for him, drive to the address at which the nurse was to be found.

Poor Nurse Edwards, sitting up in bed to receive her official visitor, looked more worn and haggard by daylight than she had done the night before. The hours which had passed had only brought to her fuller realization of the fact that she had actually seen the murderer, might have stopped him, and had failed to do so.

"But, you see, sir," she almost pleaded, as Woods took her briefly over the events of the preceding night, "I was feeling so ill. I'd had a bad fall, and I'd been badly shaken, and having my hand stitched at the hospital upset me. I felt all dazed and giddy, and going up the stairs made me feel faint. I didn't really take in what I saw, and somehow, having Mr. Godfrey come in with me, and seeing that other man, just muddled me. I can't explain properly, but I sort of confused the two, and thought the other was a friend of Mr. Godfrey's."

Looking at her bandaged head and arm, at her ashy face and heavily ringed eyes, the inspector could not find it in his heart to be hard on her. He knew well enough that with her really lay the responsibility for the murderer's escape. Godfrey was not an intimate friend, he was barely an acquaintance of Mr. Ewing's. Going into the flat as a formality, he had left it to the nurse, who was presumably familiar with her employer's friends, to speak to the stranger. The fact that Nurse had looked at the man, had said nothing, but had allowed him to depart, was, in one sense, peculiar, in another, quite comprehensible. If she were really suffering from the effects of her accident, she too must be exonerated, fatal as the result of her inaction had been.

"How did you come to be hurt?" inquired Woods, really chiefly to give himself time while he summed up the personality of this witness.

"I was crossing the road at the corner of Clevedon Street and Warr Street, on my way to the shops, sir," she began, relieved to be spared, even if only for a moment, the recalling of the scene in the flat, "and just by the chemist's shop a bicyclist came along, riding very fast, and he just seemed to crash straight into me, and over I went, and fell right on to the edge of the kerb-stone."

"At the corner of Warr Street," meditated Woods aloud. "Why, there's a big arc light there. The man ought to have seen you all right."

"Why, yes!" replied Nurse. "He couldn't help but see me. I saw him, coming along in the middle of the road. I thought he'd be well past before I crossed, so I stepped off the pavement and started off quite slowly, and he seemed to swerve, all of a sudden, and be right on top of me before I could get back."

Woods stared at her, transfixed. An idea had come flashing into his mind. Perhaps this was not an ordinary accident? The road, he knew for himself, was extremely well lighted at that corner. The nurse's account visualized for him a man deliberately altering his course in order to knock the woman down. A fast cyclist could do quite a lot of damage. The woman was bound to be hurt, and to be detained. That chemist's shop, too, was handy.

"Who picked you up, and where did you go?"

"Some people passing by helped me up. I'd struck my head, and it was bleeding. They took me in to the chemist. He did first aid, but said I wanted stitching, and I'd better go to the hospital. So he called a taxi and I went there."

Again Woods pondered. He felt that incident was premeditated. It was essential for the murderer to gain access to the flat while the nurse was out. He would need as much time as possible. An accident of this sort would effectively detain her. A bicycle was an excellent instrument, for it could inflict quite severe minor injuries, and at the same time, unlike a car, would not be easily identified.

Did you notice the man at all, before the machine hit you?

No, sir; he was riding with his head down, bent over the bars, and it was raining. I hadn't more than a glimpse of him as he hit me and over I went."

"Had you your umbrella up?"

"No, sir; I had it with me, but I'd just put it down as I meant to go into a shop on the other side of the street, and didn't want to have it up while I crossed."

"You couldn't see his face at all?"

"No, sir; he'd his hat well down on his head, and it was all done so quickly."

"Wasn't he hurt? Didn't he stop at all?"

"No, sir; he came down, of course, but as far as I know he jumped on his bike again and went straight off. I didn't see, but the people who came and picked me up said so. They said they shouted after him, but he never turned at all—just went off."

A variety of thoughts flashed through Woods's mind.

That the accident was no accident he felt sure. Had it also been collusive? Was the nurse concerned in the murder? It was possible that all was arranged with some confederate, that he had watched until she came out, that he had deliberately run her down, so that she would be detained and the field left clear for him for at least an hour, but that only *minor* injuries were inflicted, nothing which would do any serious damage but enough to give her a convincing alibi.

Concealing these suspicions, and not stopping to consider them now, for he felt this aspect must be pondered over at leisure, he decided to leave for the moment the question of the accident, and to see whether he could glean anything in other directions.

"Then you were away from the flat possibly for an hour—or longer?"

"Yes. I left just after four, and I got back about a quarter-past five."

Again Woods was startled. Times had been run very fine in this affair.

"You went up at a quarter-past five. How do you know that was the time?"

"I looked at my watch to see how late I was. I knew Mr. Ewing would be very vexed. I ought to have been back at half-past four."

"You rang, but no one answered?"

The nurse nodded, her cheeks growing very pale.

"So you went down to Mrs. Dutton?"

"Yes."

"You weren't too badly hurt to walk up the stairs and down again by yourself?"

"Oh, no! I wasn't seriously hurt, you know. Only enough to knock me up a bit."

"I see." The inspector paused. Then: "Well, now," he said briskly, aware that he could get no further from Nurse herself for the present on this point, "tell me something else. What gentlemen, or which work people, were in the habit of coming to the flat?"

Seeing her hesitation, he added: "This is just something we have to test, you know. We think that perhaps Mr. Ewing opened the door, and we want to know, first of all, who were the people he'd be likely to let in."

"Why, anyone who came, I suppose," was the reply, in rather a blank voice. "When I was out Mr. Ewing had to open the door himself. The flat was a service one, you know."

"Yes, I know," said Woods patiently; "but we don't think it altogether likely that Mr. Ewing would have let in a total stranger. Not with such a valuable collection in the house, you know, not to speak of the jewellery."

The look of complete amazement that came to Nurse Edwards's face enlightened the inspector on one point.

"Valuable jewellery?" She voiced her lack of comprehension. "Do you mean those rings and links he wore? He wouldn't bother to keep people out because of them."

Woods looked at her searchingly. "Did Mr. Ewing wear a ring, then?"

"Why, yes"—with increasing bewilderment—"he always wore two, one on each hand. One was a great big diamond, like you see some men wear—business men as a rule—and the other was a queer sort of signet ring, with a green stone, carved. He told me once that was more valuable even than the very big diamond, something to do with the carving on it, he said."

"Was it an antique?" inquired Woods.

"Why, yes, that was what he said. I remember now that was the word he used. 'It's *antique* and *unique*.' That was what he told me, he was so proud of it."

Like many nervous people, she now began to cover up her nervousness by a flow of talk, and Woods, thinking something might come of it, let her run on.

"He never took them off, during the day that is, for he was so particular about them, and I've never really seen him up and about without them. And he'd some lovely links too—jade they were, like the stuff in his cabinets only brighter, like real emeralds. But I don't think he was nervous. I don't think he'd have been *afraid* to let anyone in. Whether he'd have wanted to do so, I don't know. He didn't care for visitors, and if I were out he'd often tell me he shouldn't answer if anyone did come—not that visitors came, but sometimes there were tradespeople, and the laundry and so on. And he wouldn't have the flat left alone, for he said he didn't want people coming in when he wasn't there—the window cleaners, and people from the hotel, you know. But I should have said that was just the kind of disposition he had—not any fear of thieves—just fussiness and love of having his own way."

"Well," said Woods, "of course his collection was all insured, and we don't really think this man came for that, nor for anything to do with it. No, we think perhaps he was after the rest of the jewellery, all the good stuff he had."

Nurse Edwards merely looked at him, all astonishment, if her looks spoke truth.

"I mean," continued Woods, "the really very valuable things he had—the property of his late wife, which he kept in that black japanned box. It's valued at nearly £20,000, you know, and it has been in the flat for some time."

If he meant to startle, apparently he succeeded. Nurse looked at first stunned, then appalled, and then burst into tears.

"Well, I never knew. I never even saw a black box or anything. I don't go poking about. He never told me, and I don't think it right to keep stuff like that in a house. It's just asking for trouble, and tempting people to come in!"

"Yes," said Woods briefly, "he'd have done better to keep it at his bank, poor old man, as you say. Now, are you sure you never saw a black tin box about the place—about twenty inches by twelve?"

"Quite sure," said Nurse, trying to recover herself." I never, of course, looked in the cupboards or drawers, and I never saw it about. He never had it out as long as I've been there. I'm quite sure of that."

"You can swear to these rings you say he wore?"

"Why, yes, I've had them in my hands several times, giving them to him when he was dressing in the morning. He used to put them on his washstand shelf at night."

"They're not on the list of what was found," said Woods significantly. "They're missing, and another big solitaire diamond ring too. Know anything about that?"

"What's a solitaire ring?" asked Nurse doubtfully.

"Just the one largish diamond, set by itself—and a great big one this was too," returned Woods, glancing at his typewritten list. "Not his own gentleman's ring, you understand. One of his wife's, in fact, and one of her best."

The nurse shook her head. "I never saw one like that in the flat," she said. "Nor ever heard him speak of his wife's jewellery, I'm sure. He had the two rings I've told you of, but one was a big, square, green stone, all carved, and the other was a single stone, a diamond. But that's not the one you mean?"

"No," replied Woods. "There were two solitaire diamonds, one a man's, one a lady's. The rings were on the insurance list, and easily identifiable. Both Mr. Ewing's and the lady's are, so far, missing.

"However, let's hope the man took them," he added quite cheerfully. "That will give us one clue, anyway. Something to look for, and we've need of that."

Further questions only confirmed the evidence given by Godfrey. The stranger had only been seen by Nurse from the back. She never saw his face. She judged him to be a gentleman, tall, fairly slim, no one she knew. "But then," she explained, "I'd not been with Mr. Ewing very long, less than a couple of months, and, except for the lawyer and Dr. Ainslie, there hadn't been any gentlemen call at the flat. It wasn't either of them."

"Did you know Mr. George Fordham?"

No, she did not. He'd never been to the flat, though Mrs. George had.

Gloomily satisfied that identification was impossible, Woods finally left her, with a recommendation to remain in bed and get as much rest as she could.

He felt he had a good deal to digest in the information he had collected, but, at the moment, his chief feeling was one of disgust.

"Good heavens!" he thought, as he set out on his return to the office. "Just to think! Three people saw that man, saw him close—and none of them can identify him, or give us a decent description. The man's seen leaving the place practically red-handed, and it's no real use to us whatsoever. We've just to fall back on the old routine methods, motives—alibis—records—and I trust we'll come across something—plain routine once more."

The future, however, held more than plain routine for the inspector.

Chapter IX

THE HYPOTHESIS

All in the lust for money, to get gold.
Why, lie, rob, if it must be, murder.

The Pope, R. BROWNING.

A day later—the second day after the murder in fact—Inspector Woods sat at his desk, and surveyed the notes he had made to sum up his estimate of the case. He felt satisfaction and a vague excitement, for at last the mists were beginning to clear away. His meditations, and patient getting together of little pieces of information, were achieving something. He now had a definite conception of the crime in his mind, which he felt sure was correct.

Just as the watcher in the street had looked from the staircase into the illuminated room opposite, so Woods was seeing mentally that room, and gradually, in his imagination, events seemed to enact themselves before his eyes.

Woods was an able man. He had quick perceptions, the power of fitting things together swiftly. He had imagination, and could visualize scenes with extraordinary clearness, and sometimes he allowed his imagination to set this power to work in connexion with a crime. He had now reached this stage in the investigation of the "flat murder", as the Ewing case had come to be called, and he deliberately evoked before his mental vision the scene which his fragmentary knowledge enabled him to reconstruct.

The inquest had been held that morning, and certain points had been made clear. The medical evidence showed definitely that Simon

Ewing had been struck down where the body was found, on the hearth beside his chair. Dr. Carr's first conclusions were corroborated. Ewing had been seated in his chair, he had risen to his feet and had been struck on the head, and had pitched forward heavily to the ground. Ten or eleven subsequent blows had been showered on him as he lay prostrate. There was nothing clenched in his hands, which were uninjured, though much stained with blood from the head wounds. The position of the first heavy blow showed that he had been leaning forward, with his head slightly turned to the left.

The complete orderliness of the flat, especially of the drawing-room, showed that there had been no struggle, no alarm. After Nurse Edwards had gone out Ewing had been alone in his drawing-room, presumably writing, for the bureau was open, his writing-board laid out by his chair, and the lid off the ink-stand. A sheet of paper, with the date written on it, lay on the blotter. The pen lying beside it had made a blurred trail across the sheet. Then a ring had come at the bell, as was proved by the evidence proffered by Doreen and Anne Godfrey. The murderer had rung that bell, the time showed that clearly. The two Godfreys had heard the sound of it ringing when Henry Godfrey entered his aunt's flat. Henry himself had not noticed it, but his wife and sister were positive. Less than ten minutes later had come the crash and thud on the ceiling. It was therefore certain that whoever rang the bell of the upper flat had been admitted at that time, presumably by Simon Ewing himself.

As in the famous Wallace case, there were "no signs of forcible entry, no fingerprints, no marks of blood anywhere else in the house."

The recollection of that mysterious case recurring to his mind suddenly gave Woods pause. Would it have been possible, as had been suggested in the Liverpool murder, for the assailant to have undressed in the bathroom, gone down and committed the murder naked, and then returned to the bathroom to wash off any traces, and to dress again in his unstained clothes? The fact that the towels in the bathroom, the soap, and sponge were all dry was not conclusive, for a cunning murderer would bring whatever he needed with him, foreseeing that no clue must be left. If this theory were correct it would account for the man's appearance, his being free from bloodstains, and perfectly tidy and neat. It would also explain his descending from the upper part of the house.

Against it must be set the fact that it involved a complete change in the time-table Woods had drawn up. To undress, wash, and dress again would require probably half an hour. Therefore, if this theory were to be entertained, it followed that the ring at the bell, heard by the Godfreys, and even the crash overhead must have been deliberate fakes, intended to falsify the time of the murderer's entry and of the murder itself.

Woods felt this was probably too far-fetched, and dismissed the idea from his mind for the time being as involving too high a degree of improbability.

The question then arose, how had the murderer got in? Had he entered from the street, or had he been concealed, either in the flat itself or in the upper part of the staircase leading to the empty flats above? Henry Godfrey had said he saw no one ahead of him in the street, and certainly he had not noticed anyone going up the front steps which led both to Mr. Ewing's lower front door and to Mrs. Dutton's. It was wet and he had his umbrella, and the murderer had been up the staircase, and actually ringing at the upper bell by the time Henry was admitted to his aunt's front door.

It was therefore not impossible that the man had either simply been a little before Henry or had escaped his notice.

On the other hand, had he been waiting on the upper staircase? The objection there was that to be out of sight of the nurse leaving the flat meant that the man must have been right round the next bend in the stairs. There, if unseen, he also could not see. He would hear the door of the flat open and shut, but it was difficult to see how he could be absolutely positive that it was the nurse who had left and that there was no one with Mr. Ewing. A prolonged watch, from some place where he could definitely see who went in and out, was far more plausible.

Or—another possibility—had he gained access to the flat earlier in the afternoon, and remained hidden in that upstairs room? From there he could see both Nurse's room and down the staircase to the front door. If anyone had been able to do that, the difficulties connected with an entry made from the street door were obviated. Yet inquiries had failed to trace any pseudo workmen coming to the flat that day. The hotel staff had sent in none but the maids who habitually cleaned the flat, and Nurse Edwards was sure no one else had called. Further, this theory did not account for that ringing of the bell at five o'clock.

As to the entry from the street door, which was, as a rule, kept open in the day, but closed at night when practically no one ever called at Mr. Ewing's flat, Nurse admitted that she had left it open behind her when she went out, for she intended to do some shopping, and foresaw she would have her hands full, and would be cumbered up with her umbrella, and did not want to have to fumble for two keys—that to the lower as well as the upper door. She had, of course, shut the upper door of the flat itself.

The murderer had therefore, on the most likely hypothesis, arrived in the street and gone straight up, thus missing Henry Godfrey's arrival beneath the portico by a bare two, or at most three, minutes. He had rung the upper bell, and been admitted quite promptly. Simon Ewing had let the murderer in, and gone back with him to the drawing-room, or, possibly, had gone back to the drawing-room and left the man in the hall. Woods considered the latter possibility, because he believed, from the blotted sheet of paper on the writing-board, that Ewing had gone back to his writing, and had dropped the pen when startled in some way. That sheet of paper seemed to show that he had not made that inky blur simply when rising to answer the bell. He was not the sort of man to make a nervous movement of that sort merely at the quite ordinary sound of a ring at the door bell. Woods believed he had resumed his writing, when something unexpected had caused him to look up and drop his pen instantly, regardless of where it fell.

Now, from this Woods deduced two things. It was possible that the man who had been admitted was a workman, probably well known to him, who had come to do some repair to the flat. Nurse knew little of the tradespeople, but the electric fittings had lately been altered, some of the lamp plugs worked stiffly, and she knew Mr. Ewing had meant to have them attended to. Inquiries had been made at the shops where Mr. Ewing dealt, but, so far, no workman had come under any suspicion. All appeared to have been at jobs elsewhere. Still, Woods felt there was that possibility to be reckoned with. Indeed, a thief intending to burgle the flat for the jewellery might have discovered who were the tradespeople employed by Mr. Ewing, through the staff of the hotel, and have appeared at the flat in the guise of one of these workmen. How often were not householders confronted with men who had "come to have a look at the water pipes, or test the switchboard"? Five o'clock, though late, was not too late at such a busy season.

The other possibility, which Woods himself considered more likely to be a probability, was that the murderer was actually some person well known to Mr. Ewing, of his own station in life, whom he had readily admitted, and with whom he was on sufficiently easy terms to have bidden him wait a moment while he got off his letter.

In either case, it was clear what had happened next. Simon Ewing had been sitting in his big chair beside the fire. He had thrown down the pen, risen to his feet, and faced round to the man on the hearth. That man had struck, and knocked Ewing to the ground. The doctors had agreed that he had been fronting his assailant, that he had been felled, and probably stunned, with a heavy blow, and that he had fallen on his back on the hearth. The assailant had stooped down and pounced on him at once. The fact that nothing had been overturned or disarranged showed that Simon had not really moved from the place where he fell. The murderer probably realized the considerable crash, and he may have paused a few moments to see what would happen, or he may have proceeded at once to silence the prostrate figure. Simon Ewing had not cried out. So much was pretty certain. For almost at once, following on that fall, Nurse Edwards had arrived at the front door. She had given the time of her arrival as 5.15, and declared she stood there ringing and waiting patiently to be let in for three or four minutes without any apprehension of anything being wrong. The murderer's way of meeting that, to him, ominous ringing was known. The doctors reported that a large number of blows had been showered on the head. In the short time between Nurse's first arrival alone and her second with Godfrey, those injuries had been dealt, by a man who obviously had, in a frenzy either of self-protection or of revenge, given himself up to the utter blotting out of life.

The silence which followed upon Nurse Edwards's first attempt at entry must have told the murderer that, beyond what he could have hoped, the person at the door had gone away. As it had been some-one who actually rang, and who did not let themselves in with a key, presumably he then thought himself safe from further interruption for a while. Safe enough, in any case, to make a desperate effort to secure that for which he had committed this crime. Hastily covering the body, with the apparent intention of deceiving, if only momentarily, anyone coming into the room, and leaving it where it had fallen on the hearth, he had gone out of the room, the lights all left on behind him, and had begun his search for the jewellery. For that the jewel-lery was his object was proved, in Woods's estimation, by his being in the spare-room. While he was intent on this, he must have heard the voices of Godfrey and Nurse, either as they came up the stair or as they talked together outside the flat, followed by the sound of the key in the door. Woods could hardly imagine what that man had felt. Yet he had remained cool. He had seen that his only hope lay in a gigantic bluff, and he had brought off that bluff. Emerging without haste, without disorder, he had passed the nurse, reached the door, nodded to Godfrey—had given, in fact, a perfect representation of the ordinary visitor leaving a house, and greeting politely, but briefly, someone whom he crosses as he goes out.

Yet the speed which Anne Godfrey had detected in his steps, as he ran down the last part of the flight, gave Woods a vivid insight into the feelings which must have raged for a moment in that man's breast as he left that building.

Now, as he evoked that scene, saw the lobby, the figures in it, the man running lightly down the stairs, Woods realized definitely that there were certain very peculiar features to be considered.

The murder had been one of violence. The old man had been struck repeatedly, and about the head. A man kneeling, or leaning over the body, must have been quite deeply stained with the spurting blood. Yet the man who had emerged from the upper floor and crossed the lighted hall was not so stained. He had been turning up his coat collar and pulling down his hat, but Godfrey had noticed nothing amiss with his bare hands, or his cuffs, or his coat. Miss Godfrey corroborated this, and she had seen the man facing a bright street lamp, at close quarters.

Again, the light had been lit in the spare-room, the burnt match lay there, the candles had been moved. There were no fingerprints and no stains. The murderer had therefore worn gloves, but those gloves had been clean, they had left no bloody smears or specks. He must have slipped them on after the crime, slipped them on over his wet and sticky fingers. But, even so, it was extraordinary that he had left absolutely no drop or trace of blood in either of the rooms he had entered.

At first, Woods had considered the question of the rug. It had lain on the body, wrapped tightly round, and completely concealing it. It was stained on both sides. In the short interval which had elapsed from the moment when the Godfreys had heard the bell and the moment when Henry Godfrey lifted up that rug, it was not likely that the blood would have soaked right through the thick Persian texture. Woods believed it possible that the murderer had seized it up from the floor—perhaps it was that very action which had caused Simon Ewing to rise, startled, to his feet—had flung it over the old man, borne him to the ground, and held him stifling there until the ring at the door goaded him to smash in his victim's head. There could be no certainty of this, however, in view of Godfrey's statement that he had lifted the rug right off and dropped it down again. If he had dropped it with the fresher side down, the injuries would have stained that second side during the interval before the police arrived. Yet, to Woods, this seemed unlikely.

During his interview with Godfrey, he had vaguely formulated a theory, which he now felt himself in a position to test.

The inspector felt sure that, at close quarters, had he been crouching down so near the battered head, the murderer must have been spotted or stained on his own face. He recalled the aspect of the room and the position of the furniture. Reaching for his telephone, he called up the police surgeon.

"Dr. Carr?" he inquired abruptly, as soon as he had got the connexion. "I want to put a question to you with regard to Mr. Ewing's injuries. Could those fractures have been caused by a man standing upright, and striking at him from that position? They could? I thought so! How would he reach? Oh! Well, it's only an idea of mine, but I'll tell you if I find it holds water."

Dialling once more, he got through to Henry Godfrey's office, and asked for Henry himself.

A very ill-tempered voice soon spoke to him. Henry had been hoping for a brief respite from the police he so clearly detested.

"I'm sorry to have to ring you up at your office," said Woods apologetically. "But I thought you'd prefer I should do that rather than pay you a visit there, and there's something I wanted to get clear at once."

"Fire away, then"—very grumpily.

"I've been looking at my notes of your finding of the body. Can you recollect if you moved any of the furniture in the drawing-room before the police arrived? Did you, for instance, move any table or chair?"

A pause, while Henry evidently thought. Then he answered, rather doubtfully: "Well, I rather think, now you call it to my mind, that I did. I believe there was a chair standing somewhere near the body. I think I moved it when I pushed past the nurse to get to the body."

"Can you be more definite than that, Mr. Godfrey? Try to throw your mind back, and visualize what you saw."

"I am trying"—with irritability in every note. A pause again, and then, more decidedly: "Yes, now it's come back to me quite distinctly. There was an ordinary sort of chair, not an arm-chair, by the hearth. I pushed it back."

"In what direction?"

"Does that matter?"

"Yes, very much."

"Well, then, I took hold of it and pushed it behind me, to the right, away from the fireplace and towards the cabinet on the right."

"Thank you, sir. That was what I wanted to know."

Woods heard the receiver slammed down, but he cared nothing for Godfrey's antagonism and ill-temper. Dashing down the receiver, he seized his hat and hastened off to the flat. It had been left, after the police investigations, exactly as the police notes, reinforced by photographers, had shown it to have been originally, before the removal of the body to the mortuary. Woods went at once to the hearth. There stood the chair he had noticed, a good, solid, heavy mahogany chair, one of four ranged about the room. It had square-sided, rather sharp-ended legs. It was placed with its front legs towards the hearth, its back legs towards the middle of the room. Woods had noted the fact that Godfrey had admitted shifting the chair to get to the body. Woods did not therefore scruple to pick it up, since he knew that Henry had changed its original position. He swung it first, in his hand, feeling the weight and realizing that it was an adequate weapon. Then, reversing it, he looked carefully at the legs. The police had reported them to be stained from their close proximity to the corpse. Blood had spattered beyond this chair on to the fire-irons and coal scuttle, and on to the brown paper which had covered the waste-paper basket and the japanned box. But Woods, looking now with his theory in his mind, saw at once that the front legs were stained on their inner surfaces only. The back legs were different. One was almost clear, but the other was stained on all four sides and quite deeply. Glancing now at the underneath of the seat, he saw there, too, dark spots and blotches. Woods had found what he had been seeking. He was sure that this was the weapon. The murderer had not knelt, he had stood upright, he had kept his foot on the breast of the old man, and he had dealt blow after blow at his head with the sharp end provided by the solid leg of the chair. In that way, repeated blows would inflict the deadly injuries, while the murderer, standing at his full height, and with the seat of the chair interposed between him and his victim, would get few or no stains on either hands or face.

Woods gave a sigh of satisfaction at having put one piece of his puzzle into place. He knew now how the murder had been done. He was sure he also knew why. He believed he knew by whom. Surely, with a little more effort, he could bring his belief into line with proof?

Chapter X

THE SUSPECTS

All this trouble comes of telling truth,
Which truth, by when it reaches him, looks false.

Guido, R. BROWNING.

Returning to his office, Woods inquired for Riley, and, on hearing that the sergeant had not yet come in, he gave orders to send him up directly he should appear. Until then he occupied himself with clearing his own mind in regard to the possible suspects in the case. The weapon and method employed in the murder had been established; now Woods's theories could advance to the next stage.

On the famous "Points to be considered" in a murder case, Opportunity and Motive, he felt he had now a good deal of light.

Taking first Opportunity. It had emerged from the known details that opportunity to murder had been manufactured by the arranged absence of Nurse Edwards. Time had been provided for a thorough search of the flat, either while the owner was peaceably occupied in his sitting-room, or, as, of course, was more probable, after he had been either stunned or gagged or otherwise made harmless.

Who, then, could have taken advantage of that opportunity? Or, coming to the second point, who had sufficient motive for this crime?

Now, in considering the motive for the murder, the inspector felt certain that this was not far to seek. He did not believe that this was an elaborate or mysterious affair. Every effort had been made to investigate Mr. Ewing's life, and to search amongst his friends and surroundings for the reason why he had been attacked and killed. So far as patient investigation could go, every circumstance of his career had been laid bare. He was rich, and a widower, childless, with no near relations, and very few friends. His comparative isolation made it all the easier to trace the few intimacies he had formed. George Fordham was his wife's only nephew, the sole representative of the family, indeed. He and his wife visited Simon Ewing, but he, cripple as he was, had never been to their very modest home, away in the northern suburbs. On his side, Ewing had neither brother nor sister, neither nephew nor niece. The only connexion he possessed was apparently a very distant cousin—a Miss Nora Marshall—who lived in Scotland, and who visited her old cousin perhaps once in the course of two or three years. She had been communicated with, but could give no information. Hate or revenge were therefore ruled out. No trace of any action calling into play such motives had been found in the records of old Simon's life.

Gain, therefore, remained, and the hope of some immediate benefit.

George Fordham was the admitted heir. His uncle had never concealed the fact that he felt bound by his wife's wishes, and by her affection for her only relation. The lawyer had now produced the will, under which it appeared that Simon Ewing had left to George the entire fortune which had been his wife's, and which actually represented the bulk of his income. Simon's own capital had gone into his collection, and this he had left to the Victoria and Albert Museum.

George was, therefore, apparently the only person who stood to gain by the murder. Yet, if merely the elimination of Mr. Ewing had been aimed at, surely a less risky and clumsy method would have been employed?

For so much had been risked, and the murderer had escaped by such a rare combination of chances. The single fact that both Mr. Ewing's flat and Mrs. Dutton's shared the same portico and front steps added immeasurably to the chances of identification. Any member of

Mrs. Dutton's household might have been going up those steps simultaneously with the murderer. Henry, in fact, did very nearly do so.

This point told against the murderer having been someone who knew the local conditions. Would anyone who knew the risk he ran of recognition go up those jointly used steps? Yet that risk had been run. Would George, who had no absolute certainty that he would inherit, have done what for him was doubly dangerous?

Here, Woods considered, the motive of immediate gain must have come into play. That fatal store of jewels must have been the murderer's actual objective. For this belief, Woods thought he found confirmation in one small detail. He believed he saw the intention to acquire precious stones in the theft of the three items known to be missing. Someone coming for papers, or for plain murder, would never have dreamt of stopping to snatch off rings from a dead man's fingers. They would have hastened to their real objective. But a thief who came for jewels might, so Woods felt, have paused to make sure of even two or three pieces of what he came to steal. That he *had* done so did not seem open to doubt. Nurse Edwards had spoken most definitely of the two valuable rings Mr. Ewing wore. George Fordham, questioned on the matter, also declared he knew the rings well, and that to the best of his belief his uncle always wore them. The diamond had been Simon Ewing's wedding present from his wife, the jade one was a very valuable antique ring. These rings were missing. In addition, the list provided by the insurance company, together with a duplicate found amongst the papers in the tallboy, both gave as one item a lady's diamond solitaire ring, valued at £250, and of this, too, no trace whatever could be found. The two rings which Simon wore must clearly have been taken by the murderer from the fingers of the old man. The reason why the large solitaire ring alone was missing from the contents of the tin box remained a mystery, and yet Woods was sure it was of importance. Clues were so scarce that he could not afford to leave one tiny indication unnoticed. Every effort must be made to find out what had happened to the three rings.

Yet, at first, here too he was baffled. Search of the flat produced nothing. Circulars, taken round at once to jewellers and pawnbrokers, produced no results. Publicity in the press was to be avoided, for Woods's one hope was that the murderer might in the end do, what doubtless he would have done sooner had he dared—try to dispose of the stones. Here again the value of the jewellery was a help. For clearly anyone hoping to acquire such a mass of precious stones must have had good prospects of disposing of them. The ordinary thief could not hope to realize even a fraction of their value. Someone who had a "good practice", and knew the big fences, or who had access in one way or another to the market in precious stones, was indicated. Woods sat and mused on these lines, and as he reached this stage in his reflections the door of his office opened and Riley came in, with a distinct air of importance about him.

Woods, frowning over his notes, barely glanced up, and failed to notice the self-satisfaction radiating from his subordinate.

"Look here, Riley," began Woods, not indeed giving Riley a chance to speak. "I want you to listen to me for a moment. I've got tangled up, and I've lost the thread I thought I held. It'll help me to catch it again if I just run over my notes with you."

Riley, who naturally rather welcomed the idea of producing a sensation, was quick-witted enough to observe Woods's absorption and his rather dissatisfied knitting of the brows. He resolved to hoard up his own discovery, and to produce it at a suitably dramatic moment, for he wanted it to receive full attention, not to fall on the ungracious soil of his superior's baffled discontent.

"Right you are, sir," he answered briskly. "If you'll tell me where you've got to, we can see if I can add anything to what you know."

Disregarding this hint that Riley had something to add, Woods handed across his notes, and Riley glanced through them, while Woods commented aloud.

"You see, Riley," began the inspector, "the best clue we have, I'm convinced, lies in those rings. The murder was committed with a view to theft, the man was after that jewellery. You agree?"

Riley nodded. "Why, yes, sir, I think that's pretty certain. Though," he added reflectively, "so far, we can't find that many people knew about the jewellery."

"How far have you got in that direction?" queried Woods.

"The nurse didn't know the stuff was there. That, I think, is the truth," replied the sergeant. "She'd only been there seven weeks, and wasn't in the old man's confidence at all. And even if she had known, I don't think she'd anyone to tell. She's not engaged to any young man, has no relations in London except an old aunt, leads a very quiet life. I don't myself think the information came from her."

Woods nodded. "Yes, I think you're right," he said cautiously." I've had her record gone into. It's excellent in every way. Her accident was genuine, in the sense that she was injured in the way she described. I've seen the chemist and the doctor. She was hurt in the place, at the time, in the manner she told us."

"Well, then," said Riley, "another possible source of leakage was the insurance company. Some of their clerks knew of this inventory, knew Mr. Ewing's address, and the great value of the jewellery. But, as far as I've been able to trace the people who'd typed or filed the list, they're all above suspicion. Though, of course, one simply can't find out if they ever talked to others. It's not in human nature for people not to let their tongues run away with them a bit, and any jewel thief might know how to pick up bits of useful information. We can't say absolutely for certain that there wasn't a talk going round as to this flat full of valuable jade and jewels." He paused, and Woods intervened impatiently: "That doesn't carry us much farther. We can't trace all the gossip possibly passed about in all the various circles those insurance clerks frequented. It would be utterly impossible."

"It would," agreed Riley. "And personally I think we want to look nearer home. I've been round to everyone who came into contact with Mr. Ewing, and so far I've found three sets of people who knew what he'd got." He glanced across at Woods, then went on:" His nephew, of course, Mr. George Fordham, and his wife; the old man's lawyer, Mr. Court; and the doctor, Dr. Ainslie."

"How did the doctor come to know anything of it?"

Riley paused, and then in rather impressive tones, to show that here was a titbit indeed: "Apparently he was on quite friendly terms with Mr. Ewing. He used to go in and see him pretty frequently. He'd been in the East, and actually at the ruby mines in Burma. He and the old man used to talk about stones, and one day, about a month ago, Mr. Ewing got out this box to show the doctor some fine rubies which had belonged to his wife."

The two men looked at each other.

"That so?" said Woods, his attention thoroughly aroused.

After a moment's reflection he added: "Well, I suppose that means I must have a word with the doctor. I'll go along to him after I've seen Mrs. Fordham. I've an appointment with her first. But before I go, Riley, I just want to ask you one thing. Has it struck you that Mr. Godfrey had a professional interest in precious stones?"

Riley looked puzzled. "Well, of course, I know he's a dealer. But he could not have had anything to do with the murder. He was in the company of his relatives when it took place. Besides, the nurse, and he, and his sister saw that other man."

"I know," said Woods restlessly. "It doesn't fit, or make sense, and yet, you know, I don't trust these people. I've seen Godfrey several times now, and there's something wrong with him. He's afraid, and he's afraid of *me*. I'm dead certain he's concealing something, and something vital too."

Leaving Riley to consider this fresh subject of suspicion, Woods went off to his interview.

In going to visit Penelope Fordham, Woods was doing no more than follow up his instincts. Nothing connected her with the crime, which assuredly was not the work of a woman, nor was she any relation by blood to the murdered man.

Yet, by now, Woods was determined to disentangle every thread in the story of the dead man's family and circle. He was convinced that there he would get at the proof which he hoped would lead him to the conviction of the murderer. So he made his way to the tiny maisonette in the neighbourhood which liked to be called Highgate, but which might more truthfully be described as Kentish Town. Familiar as he now was with Simon Ewing's flat, its beautiful contents and luxurious fittings, and recalling, as he did, the wealth which he knew the dead man had possessed, Woods could not fail to be struck by the contrast afforded by Penelope Fordham's surroundings.

She herself had answered his ring, for she had no maid, and as she asked him into the tiny sitting-room, she began to take off the coloured apron which she had worn while she had been preparing a meal. She was shabbily dressed, and Woods felt an impulse of compassion as he looked at her slender figure, noticed her tired eyes and general air of constant effort and strain induced by the struggle which life evidently involved for her.

Indeed, as he drew up a chair to the table, got out his notebook, and mechanically entered up a few formal particulars, his mind dwelt on the various young women with whom this case had brought him into contact—Penelope herself, Doreen, and Anne Godfrey. Anne, the unmarried one, had struck him as being the happiest and most contented. She might be solitary, but at least, as her calm, steady manner seemed to show, she had found peace in her independence. Both Doreen and Penelope, he realized, were not fortunate in their marriages, for both had married unsatisfactory men. Godfrey was superficially attractive, but Woods, being far from a fool, had already seen beneath the surface, and was fully aware of the violent temper, the sullen irritability, which made the Godfrey home an uncomfortable place; though, as Godfrey had, up to the present, been fairly prosperous, their household had an air of comfort, if not of harmony.

Here, in George Fordham's ménage, there was apparently neither peace nor plenty. The maisonette was tiny and very sparsely furnished. The cheap neighbourhood would only have been chosen by those who had little to spend. George, as Woods knew, was unsuccessful in his work, and the face and manner of his wife seemed to show he had proved a failure as a husband.

"I've come to see you chiefly as a matter of routine, Mrs. Fordham," began the inspector. "I just want to hear from yourself whether you can give me any facts about Mr. Ewing." He paused, but Penelope made no answer. She had sat down opposite to him and was gazing at the hands she had clasped in her lap, with an apparent determination not to meet the inspector's eyes.

"I understand," Woods went on, "that you used occasionally to visit Mr. Ewing?"

"Yes, I did," replied Penelope briefly.

"When you saw him, did you notice anything with regard to the jewellery he was in the habit of wearing?"

After a moment's hesitation, Penelope answered, still keeping her gaze on her lap:" I don't think I quite know what exactly you mean by his jewellery?"

"What rings, if any, would you say he generally wore?"

Still as she sat, Penelope could not altogether keep from a faint stiffening of her pose as she answered:

"My uncle always wore two rings, an antique carved jade one, and a diamond one."

"Did you ever see him with a big single-stone, diamond ring which had belonged to his wife?"

"No."

"Have you ever heard him mention such a ring?" Now at last Penelope did look up, and fixing her large dark eyes on Woods's face she answered quite steadily:

"Yes, I know there was a ring of that sort. It had belonged to his mother-in-law, my husband's grandmother. She gave it to my husband's Aunt Ada, Mr. Ewing's wife."

"Did your aunt wear that ring in her lifetime?"

"No; she always wore her own diamond cluster. Her engagement ring it had been. But why are you asking all this, Inspector?"

"Because," said Woods, determined to come out into the open, and perceiving behind Penelope's manner that there was something in her mind concerned with this ring, "we know Mr. Ewing had such a ring in his possession, and we know it is missing, as indeed are the other two. I've every reason to believe that the murderer took them all, and it's one of the things which may put us on his trail."

At these words a deep crimson flush spread over Penelope's face, and then, receding, left her ashy pale. Her lips looked almost blue, the dark circles beneath her eyes deepened until they were brown against her pallor. With manifest effort she shut her lips tightly, and sat, as if transfixed with horror, still gazing at her companion.

Woods was startled, then, anxious to induce her to speak, for now he saw clearly she had some knowledge which had hitherto been kept from him:

"Mrs. Fordham," he said earnestly, "do believe me in what I'm going to say. Tell me anything you know about this ring. I see you do know something. Believe me, it's always best to tell the truth. Don't keep things back which we ought to know."

He ceased, fearing to say too much, for a struggle was clearly going on in Penelope's mind, and he knew that silence is often effective in inducing others to speak.

He judged correctly, for Penelope, scarcely seeming to listen to what he had said, suddenly rose to her feet.

"Inspector, I'll do what I suppose I ought to have done before. But I didn't know you'd find out about that lady's ring." As she spoke she turned to a writing-table standing in the window. From it she took a shabby little leather box, marked "Stamps", and opening it she took from it and laid on the table the missing ring. "You see," she added, with a faint smile, "the murderer didn't take it, Inspector." Woods was quick in recovering his self-possession.

"Do you mean *you* did, Mrs. Fordham? Or was this given to you?"

He waited for her to answer, but he knew before she spoke that it had not been given to her, or she would have been wearing it openly.

"No," said Penelope, "it wasn't given to me. I suppose I did take it." She added drearily, as if now she hardly cared what anyone thought of her: "I've a sort of explanation to give, but it's a very poor one, and I don't know what you'll have to do when I tell you."

Woods said nothing, but waited for her to go on.

"I went to see my uncle on the evening of the 20th—"

"Of the 20th?" interrupted Woods at once. "The evening of the murder? Why haven't you come forward and told us this before?"

"Because of the ring," said Penelope. "If you'll listen, I'll explain. No one has known, up to now, but the very afternoon of the murder I went to see my uncle. I got there just after four o'clock. Nurse had gone out. Uncle Simon came and let me in. He wanted me to post some parcels. He told me one of them was this ring, and he was sending it to a distant cousin of his who was going to be married. I was awfully upset. The ring came from George's side of the family. We'd looked on it as a family possession and Uncle Simon was giving it away to one of his own cousins!" She paused, as if expecting comment, but none came. She went on: "It was a wet night, and the post office was very full. I couldn't get into the door even, the queue was right out into the street. I began to wait, but it was cold, and I suddenly thought I wouldn't stay. So I came home. I pretended to myself I'd post it next day. Then, later that night, the police sent for George. They told him Uncle Simon was dead. He went off, and came back in an awful state. He was dreadfully upset. We're very poor, Inspector, and he was suddenly afraid—he thought he—Uncle Simon—might not have left him—have left him the money. Everything turned on that for us. He came back in an absolute state of nerves. He kept on saying his uncle was dead, and he didn't know about the will. Uncle Simon didn't like George—perhaps he'd left him nothing, and then we were done for.

"I didn't tell him about the ring. But I thought that his uncle was dead, and no one knew he'd given it to me to post. I didn't think it would even be missed. I knew it was worth quite a lot, and I felt desperate. I felt we *must* have just that, in case we never got anything else. It ought to have been ours in one sense—it never belonged to his family at all." She broke off, and, as if aware of her growing agitation and effort to justify herself: "But, of course, that's nothing to do with it. I know I'd no right to it at all. I know I've really stolen it. But I haven't dared to own up. It's been awful, but I couldn't face doing that. I just made up my mind to keep silent, but I told myself that if anyone asked, if you, the police, were to ask, I'd tell the truth, and now I have."

She came to a sudden stop, as if she were at the end of her powers.

Woods looked across at her and spoke quite gently.

"Well, Mrs. Fordham, I'm very glad you have told me the truth. Just tell me this now. Do you know what the time was when you left the flat?"

"It was getting on for five o'clock," replied Penelope. "Uncle Simon commented on it, because Nurse ought to have been back and wasn't—we both noticed the time by the clock."

"Nearly five o'clock," said Woods, with a subtle change in his voice. "Then you left only just before the murderer arrived. He went up at about five. That makes a difference, you know."

He paused, then went on:

"I'm not quite sure what the position is about the ring from the legal point of view. You see, your uncle was dead before you could have got that parcel into the post. Possibly the ring really belongs to your husband after all. I don't know."

Penelope gazed at him in horror. She had not, until that moment, grasped how quickly the murder had followed upon her leaving the flat.

"Oh!" she gasped. "That's awful. To think I went away and left him, and the man went straight up and found him! I hadn't understood that. I thought somehow from what George said that it all happened later—nearer six than five! And I haven't read the papers. I couldn't— those things make me feel sick."

She looked, indeed, almost as if she would faint now, but Woods, intent on this new factor in the case, paid no attention.

"You left just before five," he mused. "Now, I wonder if the man knew that? He ran it pretty fine, between you and Mr. Godfrey. Did you see anyone outside?"

"No, no one," replied Penelope, trying to rally her strength and anxious to placate the inspector. "I just put up my umbrella and went off. There was no one in the street that I noticed."

"Which way did you go?" inquired Woods.

"I turned to the right, towards the Earls Court Road. I meant to go to the post office opposite the Tube Station. I didn't meet anyone in Clevedon Street, I'm quite sure."

"To the right? Then didn't you meet Mr. Godfrey? He was on his way from the Tube, you know, and would be coming from that direction."

Penelope shook her head. "I never saw him. But"—rather doubtfully—"he might have been the other side of the road. I had my umbrella up. I didn't see across the road—not very clearly, anyhow. But I certainly don't remember seeing anyone at all. The street was quite empty to my recollection."

Woods considered for a moment. Then, glancing up from his notebook, he at last noticed the girl's white cheeks and shaking hands. Horrified lest she should faint away, he spoke at once, with his kindest and most soothing manner.

"Well, I won't bother you about that, Mrs. Fordham. I'm afraid this has been a distressing business for you. I'll not stay longer. I'll take the ring with me." He picked it up as he spoke. "I'll have to make a report, of course, explaining how it came to be in your possession. Can you, by the way, produce the paper in which it was done up?"

Penelope had been reassured by his words and voice. A little colour came back into her cheeks. "Yes, I can," she said, speaking with less effort. "I kept the wrapping. I thought sometimes perhaps I'd just do it up and send it off, and people would think it had been delayed in the Christmas rush."

She fumbled in the drawer of the writing-table, and produced a neatly folded little packet of brown paper, with a string and some broken seals attached.

Woods took them, thanking her, and stowed the little parcel away. He wondered secretly that she had apparently never grasped the importance to her of preserving that paper, with its seals, which probably bore the impress of the old man's fingers, for it was really the proof that Mr. Ewing had actually done up that parcel and handed it to the girl. Without it, Penelope had no shadow of proof that she had not simply stolen the ring from the flat itself—an implication which would actually involve her in suspicion of murder.

Though convinced that the girl before him had no part or lot in the murder, Woods yet, by some curious impulse born perhaps of the connexion hitherto subsisting in his mind between this ring and the others which were still missing, turned back, in the very act of opening the door.

"The other rings, Mrs. Fordham? You haven't seen them? Do you know anything about them?"

"No," replied Penelope firmly, conscious that here at least she was on the safe ground of innocence. "Uncle Simon was wearing them that evening as usual. I noticed them as we did up the parcels. I didn't know until you told me just now that they were missing."

"Yes," replied Woods, "they were missing when the body was found, at 5.20—so there's no doubt that they, at any rate, were taken by the murderer."

He was preparing to go, when Penelope, summoning up her courage, asked him:

"Why did you say that the ring—the big diamond one—might be my husband's after all by right, Inspector?"

Woods glanced at the clock. "Well, Mrs. Fordham, your husband was seeing Mr. Court, your uncle's lawyer, this afternoon, and I can tell you now that he'll have heard that Mr. Ewing left the whole of your late aunt's very considerable property to him."

Penelope stood speechless, relief deprived her of words. She could only feel in one flash that here at least was the end of the poverty which had been so heavy in its pressure. The inspector, seeing her lost to the consciousness of his presence, decided to trouble her no further. He went quietly away, and prepared for the next interview he had arranged—namely with Dr. Ainslie. One thing had now been made clear. The murder had taken place when it did because it was committed at the first opportunity when Simon Ewing was left alone. As he walked away, Woods felt a glow of satisfaction, for he perceived the immense importance of this piece of information. Indeed he felt he had advanced enormously within the past half-hour. He only hoped his coming interview might prove equally fruitful.

Chapter XI

THE DOCTOR

The manner that offends, the rude and rough.

Guido, R. BROWNING.

Making his way up Clevedon Street, Woods reflected how easily the owners of house property had adapted themselves to new conditions. These large, solid, old-fashioned houses were, not so long before, looked on as white elephants. Now, with the decrease in the number of maids kept by the ordinary householder, had come a revolution in the style of living. People wanted flats or maisonettes, run by one or at most two maids. In a residential neighbourhood such as this, there was an immense demand for this type of accommodation. Property owners had seized their opportunities, and the vast majority of these large houses were now divided up into three or more sets of flats, each bringing in a good rental. Clevedon Street had quite recently suffered transformation on these lines. An enterprising individual had bought up five or six of the houses on one side, whose leases had fallen in, and converted them. Bright paint, new doors, a general air of having started in life afresh, characterized them.

Dr. Ainslie had been one of those coming to take up their habitation in these new quarters. His plate was affixed to the door of one of the most recently decorated flats. His car, a smart new one, was drawn up before the kerb. When Woods was admitted to the house and shown into the waiting-room, he observed that everything within was in keeping. New curtains, new carpets, and, if he were not mistaken, new furniture, all seemed resplendent with freshness.

"H'm! Didn't I hear he'd recently married?" meditated Woods, as, glancing from the window at the sound of the front door banging, he beheld a very smart and elegant young woman run down the steps and across the pavement, and get into the car.

As he stood watching her drive off, his gaze wandered across the street. He noticed that this flat, though not exactly opposite No. 5, commanded a good view of that front door.

He was recalled from his meditations by the entry of the maid into the room behind him. She came to tell him the doctor was free now, and would see him.

Woods found himself facing a man whose rather grim, tight-lipped face at first took him by surprise. Somehow, he had unconsciously visualized the owner of such fresh, bright quarters, and the husband of such a gay young woman, as likely to be a smiling and cheerful individual. His attention caught by the unexpected character of the man he now faced across the formal desk, he gave more study than he had anticipated to the personality with whom he now came in conflict.

For the doctor was in no accommodating mood. His blue eyes looked frostily at the inspector, his stiff attitude betokened no friend-liness, and his voice was markedly cold as he inquired what was his visitor's business.

Woods came to the point at once.

"I asked you to see me, Dr. Ainslie, because I understand you not only attended Mr. Ewing in the capacity of his medical man, but you also knew him personally as a friend."

"That is so." The doctor was not expansive.

"How long had you known him?"

"I have attended him for the past five years."

"Mr. Ewing suffered from rheumatoid arthritis?"

"He did."

"Was he able to walk about?" persevered Woods, determined not to let his growing annoyance get the better of his politeness.

"Yes, when he was not suffering from one of his bad attacks."

"When did you last see him?"

"On the morning of the 20th."

"The morning of the murder, that is to say?"

The doctor merely nodded.

"Was he in bed on that occasion?"

"He was."

"But you instructed the nurse that he might get up that afternoon?"

"Yes."

Woods really felt his patience wearing thin.

"Would he have been able to walk across the room?"

"Certainly he would."

"Now, Dr. Ainslie, coming to your more personal relations with Mr. Ewing, did he ever discuss his private affairs with you?"

"No," replied the doctor, "he did not."

"Yet I understand you were one of the few friends he possessed?"

"I was one of his friends. I don't know if he had few or many."

"Did he ever mention to you the terms of his will?"

"'No, certainly not."

"Though he asked you to be one of the witnesses of it?"

This time the doctor's frigid calm was broken. He looked faintly annoyed.

"Yes, that is so, of course. But he merely asked me to witness it, without going into any particulars as to its purport."

" Quite so," said Woods, feeling that he was not even beginning to get into touch with his companion. "But I believe Mr. Ewing did discuss one portion of his property with you? I mean, of course, his late wife's collection of jewels."

"Discuss isn't quite the correct term, Inspector. Mr. Ewing happened to know I had been in Burma at the ruby mines. I had a post there for a while. He also knew that I took a general interest in precious stones, and have made a study of them. He showed me some very fine stones he himself possessed. I should say that is not at all what is meant by your phrase 'discussing his property'?"

"Well," said Woods patiently, "perhaps I expressed myself badly. What I wanted to know was whether you were in point of fact aware of the extent and value of this jewellery?"

" Oh yes. Mr. Ewing had consulted with me over the valuation made by the insurance company, and I had gone through every item of the list with him."

"Would you agree with the estimate of the insurance company that the total value of the jewellery was £20,000?"

"I think that was a sound valuation for insurance purposes," returned the doctor, determined to be noncommittal. "One or two of the items were perhaps worth rather more, in my estimation, but the total was near enough, and the premium high enough," with a faint indication of unbending.

"I'm obliged to ask you, doctor," went on Woods, with every effort to be conciliatory," whether you spoke of this jewellery to other people?"

"I really couldn't say," returned the doctor coolly. "Mr. Ewing made no pretence of showing me the stones privately, as it were. I'm not, of course, in the habit of gossiping with all and sundry. On the other hand, I have certainly spoken of Mr. Ewing's things to one or two experts—persons like myself who are interested in precious stones."

"Such as?" queried Woods.

"Oh, a man I met at my club who is a dealer in rather a big way— and one of the men at the geological museum. I can't call anyone else to mind at the moment."

"Your wife, perhaps, has heard you speak of the matter?"

"Certainly she has. As I tell you, there was no secrecy in the matter whatever. And"—anticipating Woods's next question—"I dare say it is possible she has mentioned it to her friends in her turn. If you are trying to discover from me who knew that Ewing possessed this jewellery, you now know as much as you're likely to find out, Inspector."

"You can't, in short," said Woods, keeping his temper, "give me any help in tracing how the knowledge of his having any jewellery, on the face of it unlikely in the case of a man, got about?"

"I'm not aware that such knowledge had got about, much less how it did so."

Woods felt it useless to continue in the face of this obstructive attitude. He rose to go, believing he would do no good by prolonging the conversation, when, to his surprise, the doctor, apparently relenting as he saw Woods meant to pursue the matter no further, hesitated, glanced swiftly at the inspector, and then added suddenly:

"But I can tell you of one thing which may be of use to you."

Woods paused expectantly.

"There was a fellow lurking about here on and off for a week or more before the murder."

This was indeed news, and the inspector sat down again and listened intently.

The doctor, glancing at him again, as if to see the effect of his words, went on:

"I'm backwards and forwards here at various odd times of the day and night, and I've had occasion to notice this man loitering about the street, near my door, once or twice. One night I'd been called out rather late in the evening—I was back here with my car just on midnight—and I found a man leaning against my railings. I was going to ask him what he was up to when he moved off."

"Can you describe him?"

"No, not very clearly. He wore an overcoat, and a soft hat. I'd say from his build he was youngish. Well dressed. I couldn't see his face."

"You saw him more than once in the neighbourhood?"

"Yes, I think I did," rather slowly.

"When was that?"

"I think I saw him again on the late afternoon of the day of the murder itself, at about 4.30."

Woods stared at him, petrified, as he reflected on the immense importance of this new statement.

Here was another prospect of obtaining a little more information. Was George Fordham hanging about and watching in the street at that hour? Would he have taken such a risk of being identified? Quick as a flash Woods saw that it was just possible for a reckless man to be daring enough. Fordham might be quite an unfamiliar figure to the doctor, in view of the bad terms on which he was with his uncle. It was essential to try to test Ainslie's story.

Seeing the effect he had produced, the doctor went on, with a sort of grim relish, as if now he had once brought himself to speak he wished to show he had something after all worth saying: "I came home about 4.30 that day. It was very wet and these side streets were empty. I came round the corner of the road rather quickly, and as I shot round I thought I saw this same fellow lurking again in front of my door. Actually I was not coming to my own house. I meant to get in a call before tea to a patient living next door. The man moved along as I came up in my car and, I thought, went into the block I intended to visit."

"Yes?" said Woods, quite eagerly, as the doctor paused.

"Well—that was all," replied Ainslie coolly. "I went up to my patient's flat, on the first floor, but there was no sign of anyone.

I concluded that either I'd mistaken the house or it might have been someone looking for Mr. Hetherington—the artist, you know, who lives on the top floor there."

Woods was silent for a moment. He must go warily.

"What time did you leave your patient?"

"Oh, I don't exactly know," carelessly. "I imagine I was there half an hour or so."

"You saw no one about when you left?"

"No."

"No one in the street? No one going in opposite?"

"No, no one."

"Then you went—?" Woods paused expectantly.

"I went straight along back to my own home. I was having tea with my wife when Mrs. Godfrey came running across for me."

"Now, this man you saw hanging about. Do you think he was anyone you had seen before? That is to say, elsewhere than in the street?"

Woods spoke with emphasis and waited eagerly for the reply.

When it came, however, he was disappointed.

"No, I'm pretty certain I'd never seen him. He didn't strike me as anyone I'd ever seen before."

"You say he walked away from you? His figure and build didn't remind you of anyone?"

"No, no one," impatiently.

"And I suppose he wasn't any of the men living in the neighbourhood who were likely to be about here? Anyone you see going about this street?"

"Well, I've not lived in this street very long myself. I used to lived in Cannon Square, half a mile away. I only moved here a couple of months ago when these flats were constructed. I married then and wanted bigger quarters than my old ones. I'm not very familiar, therefore, with the inhabitants round about. But I'd never noticed the man before, and I certainly believe that I did see him on these two occasions, loitering about near my door, in the actual week before the murder—and, as of course you realize, on each occasion he was near Mr. Ewing's house."

Woods reflected. "Did you notice anything about his walk as he moved away?"

The doctor shook his head. "He went off rather quickly when my car drew up. I don't think he expected me to turn up, and I came round the corner here rather fast. I'm certain he didn't want me to see him. He made off the moment he saw my car stopping in front of the house."

"Why didn't you give the police this information earlier, Dr. Ainslie?" Woods asked abruptly.

The doctor's face hardened once more, and he shrugged his shoulders.

"I expected you to ask that, Inspector. Well, I really didn't feel it in the least necessary. I just noticed this fellow. I paid no special attention to him. I can't describe him for you. Really I didn't feel I'd anything of sufficient importance with which to waste your time and mine."

The last words were uttered with emphasis. Woods felt they were meant to convey the impression that the doctor's time was valuable— more so than his information. He was determined, however, not to be brow-beaten, and therefore spoke firmly.

"I think you must realize, Dr. Ainslie, that is not the view we should be likely to take. This is a case of murder. It is the duty of every citizen to give any information which may be of value to the police. It is for us to decide what is the exact value of anything we are told."

Ainslie's cheeks flushed, and he spoke angrily.

"I don't consider it any part of my duty as a citizen to help to bring a man to the gallows."

Woods looked at him in astonishment, then a sudden impulse apparently drove the doctor to explain his heat.

"I won't conceal from you, Inspector, what my views are. I am one of those who disapprove of capital punishment."

A silence followed. Then Woods spoke slowly.

"Well, I won't take up any more of your time, Dr. Ainslie. I can only repeat—the view of the police will be that you ought to have come forward with this information at once."

The doctor, bright spots burning in his cheeks, merely stretched out his hand to press the bell. Either he repented of his outburst, or he felt Woods had shown considerable forbearance, for he suddenly drew it back, and, as the inspector picked up his hat and turned to go, Ainslie spoke once more, this time with obvious effort.

"I must beg your pardon, Inspector, if I have spoken too forcibly. I feel rather strongly, and I've perhaps allowed myself to be influenced by the views I hold. But I felt most reluctant to come forward and offer any information, though I decided to tell you what I had seen when you came to me with your inquiries."

Woods felt unable to respond very cordially to this flag of truce. Indeed he was not altogether sure if it were meant to be one or not.

However, he did not really wish to antagonize this strange, forcible man, and in the effort to meet him half-way he bethought him of one other point he wished to ascertain.

"This artist you spoke of—Mr. Hetherington—can you tell me anything about him?"

"Why, yes, as it happens I can. I've run into him once or twice since this affair. He is a newcomer like myself. He only moved in a week ago. I've run across him once or twice since, and we've exchanged a few words. Naturally this affair in our road has made neighbours talk together rather more than one usually does."

"You didn't mention this man to him?"

"No, I did not," rather briefly.

"Well, I shall have to see what he has to say. We may find, of course, that the man was a bona fide person known to Mr. Hetherington, and visiting him quite normally that evening."

Woods turned to go, and as he did so he just caught a look which flashed across the doctor's face as at last he rang the bell for the maid to show the inspector out.

"He doesn't think so himself!" thought Woods, passing down the hall. His eye fell on a pile of letters, just come by the post, which the maid had been in the act of putting out on the hall table. As his keen eye fell upon them Woods recognized the type.

"A nice packet of bills coming in! Well, a new wife and a new home runs a man in for a good bit, I expect," and, with the reflection that to be a bachelor perhaps had compensations, he went out into the streets, and began to sort out his impressions.

If this man had been seen by the doctor he might have been seen by others, some possibly who could give a better description than Dr. Ainslie had done. A house-to-house canvass of the street was indicated, and for that Woods could enlist the services of subordinates. He himself had other work to do.

Returning to his office, he sent for Riley, and briefly explained to him the result of his interview and the importance of the new development.

Riley, who was very shrewd in his own way, paused for a moment before departing on his errands, and said:

"Do you notice, sir, how all the men we come across in this case seem to be hard up? I've been getting all the information I could from the people at the hotel. The porter there knows all the gossip of the street. I've heard about Dr. Ainslie. He's tried to cut too much of a dash, from all they say. Plunged pretty deeply when he moved in here and blossomed out. Then Mr. Godfrey. As you and I know, he's hard pressed for cash—business bad, and all that. Mr. Fordham hasn't a bean to bless himself with—or hadn't till now. And that artist's worse off than either of them. Living just anyhow, the porter tells me. The char who cleans for him says there's nothing much beyond bread and cheese goes into the flat!"

Woods nodded. "That may well be, and yet it can all be accounted for quite easily perhaps. The doctor has had to make a bit of an outlay. He won't do well in a neighbourhood like this if he doesn't have a prosperous-looking house and a good car, and so on. He's had to incur expense, and he's unlucky in the time he's chosen. People have been economizing, so the papers say, on their doctors and their nursing-homes. Harley Street is as hard hit as the Stock Exchange. I suppose Dr. Ainslie has gambled on the chance that recovery is setting in now. Mr. Godfrey and this artist, Hetherington, are in the same boat. They're all in the 'luxury' trades, as they're called. When money is short, jewels and pictures are easily done without. People just don't buy. As for Mr. Fordham, I imagine there, too, he might have kept his end up if the bottom hadn't dropped out of trade. Big firms aren't putting up buildings, no one wants that floor-covering stuff. I expect his commission has simply fallen away to nothing. But it's all what you might have expected in a locality of this sort, really. The people who live round here are just the class which has been hardly hit."

"Yes," said Riley, with a slight sigh. "Yes, I suppose that's so. Makes you realize how these people look all right, prosperous, nice families, nice homes, and then you get to know the inside of their affairs, and they've less security than you or I."

Woods nodded his agreement with this piece of moralizing, and then saying, "Well, you get on with those inquiries, Riley," began to clear off the arrears in routine work before tackling the next piece of work on the case, which was to be the attempt to trace George Fordham's whereabouts at 4.30 on the 20th.

Chapter XII

THE WIFE

What an he were foul,
Blood drenched and murder crusted head to foot?
Miscalculation has its consequence.

Guido, R. BROWNING.

The funeral was over, and the small band of mourners had struggled back to their cars through the crowd of morbid sightseers.

"Well! That's over, thank God!" grunted George Fordham, flinging himself back and removing his hat.

"And now, Nell, I only hope to goodness you'll take off that dismal look and cheer up a bit!"

His wife saying nothing, he looked furiously at her, and burst out:

"You're enough to sicken any man! What do you want to pretend to be gloomy about? You know, as well as I do, that we're going to be all right now—and there's no need to try and work up any sorrow over an old man who never did *us* any good!"

"He didn't do us any harm either," returned Penelope briefly.

"Oh! Didn't he? You and I differ over that. He did me the deuce of a lot of harm when he wouldn't even lend me £100 when I wanted it! And the old brute rolling in money all the time! Deserved all he got, I think!"

Penelope turned even paler with disgust at these words. She longed to break out herself, and express some of the contempt and revulsion she felt at such words spoken with such an indecent lack of the commonest compassion. She looked at her husband's dark face, at his heavy flushed cheeks, and refrained. George had fortified himself for the occasion with much whisky, and his temper was not one to provoke.

Sitting back and controlling herself, Penelope began to think. Could she, should she, bear with this man any longer? She had long since lost the affection so mistakenly bestowed on him. She had stuck to him from loyalty. Things had gone so badly with George. He had lost his jobs, found it so hard to get others. They had grown poorer and poorer. He had sunk from a decent post in a big accountant's office to the precarious agency. Even that job she knew he had been on the verge of losing. She couldn't have deserted him when everything was against him. Now, however, loyalty, pity, determination to stick to him as long as he needed help need not influence her. George was going to be rich—was so already. Where another woman might have reflected that at last she was to reap some benefit, come into the haven of peace and plenty after very stormy seas, Penelope's thoughts ran in quite opposite directions. George would not need anyone to stand by him now. He would get along well enough with a good income and plenty of capital, if he chose to realize it. She need sacrifice herself no longer. Suddenly Penelope's mind was made up. She would go, she would leave him. Life with him was not tolerable; she would rather be free and try to begin again by herself. She raised her eyes and looked at him. He was staring in front of him, he too, perhaps, thinking of the change now coming in their lives, though to him, clearly, the future was bright with the fulfilling of desire. Something in his appearance, as she made ready to tell him of the decision she had come to, checked the words on Penelope's lips. He seemed to her scrutinizing eyes to look ill, worn, and haggard. Was it simply that, having resolved to cut herself adrift, she saw him with fresh eyes, as a stranger might?

Or had the prospect, now happily vanished, of being cast adrift once more in a world which had not the slightest wish to employ him, really aged and altered him?

In either case Penelope, while still feeling deep within herself the knowledge that she had come to a final resolution, while still at heart determined that their life together must end, decided that she would not fulfil her first impulse, she would not tell George now. She would be patient a little longer. In a week or two, when he had settled himself more securely into his new prosperity, she would speak to him, but for the moment things should go on as before.

She clung to this resolution, just as in the past she had kept herself from collapse on many an occasion, despite the strain which the next few days imposed upon her.

George was anxious to be rid of their old life as speedily as might be. There was nothing to prevent him from launching out at once on the tide of his new fortune. He was Simon Ewing's only near relation, and he was the principal beneficiary under the will. Friends, accordingly, were readily forthcoming, though for the immediate present no steps could be taken to get rid of Mr. Ewing's belongings. Mr. Court, however, informed him that he could, of course, have access to the flat, now freed from police supervision, and that there would be no objection to his deciding at once which of the contents of the flat he would keep, and which should be disposed of as soon as the legal formalities had been completed.

The collection of jade had been bequeathed to the nation, and as it was clear that objects of such value could not be left in an empty flat, the museum to which they had been left had been authorized to move them. Packers were to be sent in the next day. Meanwhile each cabinet had been securely sealed up.

Penelope herself felt that she would never willingly have taken any of the contents of that flat into her own home. She was sure that the mere sight of the handsome bureau, or of the walnut tallboys, would always have recalled to her their dreadful associations with violent death. She would have hated to find herself looking at their polished surfaces, and perhaps suddenly remembering the scene of which they once had formed the setting and witnesses.

As she had decided, however, that she would not share George's new home, she did not feel it necessary to voice her feelings. George himself had clearly no such fancies. To him these were old family possessions, kept from him by an interloper, now at last his own. For such seemed to be the mental attitude he had adopted towards the dead man. He spoke now, always, as if Simon had had no right to any of the goods he had enjoyed. They had come from his wife, but they were a family inheritance, and George, as true representative of that family, was, and it appeared to his vision had always been, the rightful possessor. Penelope made no attempt to point out to him the oddity of this view. She no longer cared to make any effort where George was concerned. He could be as wrong-headed as he chose now, he was no longer her concern.

She had fixed in her mind the day when she would tell him that she was going away. She did not know whether he would be surprised, or whether he would object. To avoid any scenes of temper or worse, she determined to give him no chance. She would go when he was out, and leave him a letter. Until then she would try to make their last few days together peaceable, if they could not be agreeable.

So she fell in with all his suggestions, even agreed to visit the flat with him and inspect the furniture. She had never known the history of any of the handsome pieces, did not know which were really old family things. George himself had so rarely visited his uncle that he had forgotten what was there. He was, apparently, quite pleased at the prospect of inspecting the premises, as he put it. So, though she shrank from seeing once more a place which now had such horrible associations, Penelope, after brief hesitation, found herself falling in with George's suggestion.

She had an appointment for the next afternoon—a Saturday—with the dentist, who lived actually in the next road to Clevedon Street. George had a visit to pay to the lawyer, who also lived nearby. It was arranged that they would meet at the flat. He had been given the keys of the lower and upper doors, and those he now handed over to Penelope. They were both to be at the flat at four o'clock; they would go through the rooms carefully, and go in afterwards to tea with Mrs. Dutton and Anne. George promised not to be late, and Penelope was always a punctual person.

Penelope came out of the Tube station at Earls Court and crossed the road. She began to make her way in the direction of the dentist's house. Had anyone been observing her they would have noticed her slow and hesitating steps. She reached the big Cromwell Road, and paused again. Then her eye fell upon a telephone booth at the corner. She went into it, and put a call through to the dentist.

"Mr. Howes? Mrs. Fordham speaking. I'm so sorry, but I can't keep my appointment. I'm afraid I'm not feeling very well. Oh no! nothing much, and I'm ashamed not to come, but I've a very bad headache, and I'm afraid if I did come and you had to hurt me I'd turn faint or something silly. If I can come another day I think I'd better. That really is all right? Thank you so much, and I'm so very sorry to be so stupid."

She came out of the telephone booth and looked around. It was only a quarter-past three. She turned and began to walk towards the flat in Clevedon Street. Kensington was a long way from Kentish Town. It being Saturday afternoon, the shops in the district were all closed. It was bitterly cold, with a harsh, biting wind, and a few flakes of snow drifting down occasionally, and Penelope had no wish to loiter about the streets for half an hour.

She could think of no one to go and see. Then she remembered Mrs. Dutton. She did not really know her very well, but in the course of the investigations had necessarily been brought in contact with the family. She and George were to go in there later for tea. Surely Mrs. Dutton would not mind if she dropped in there to wait until four o'clock? If she and Anne Godfrey were both out, so much the better. The porter, who knew her quite well, would be sure to let her in. So she turned towards Clevedon Street.

As she reached the steps which led up to the flats, however, she paused. She was facing the windows of Mrs. Dutton's sitting-room, and the window nearest the front door was open. From it came the sound of voices in rapid conversation, and Penelope distinctly heard Mrs. Dutton's voice saying:

"Oh! but, Inspector, I really can't tell you anything…" The rest of the sentence was lost. Penelope, who had raised her hand to ring the bell, let it drop. Cautiously she tried from where she stood to peer inside the window, but she could make nothing of it. After a brief pause, she did hear a man's voice, quite clearly, and recognized Woods's tones, sharp, incisive, and unmistakable. The sound brought before her at once the recollection of the last time she had heard that voice. Her cheeks burnt with the remembrance it brought. She thought of the confession she had been obliged to make on that occasion, and was filled with an intense determination to avoid him. She could not do that if she once entered Mrs. Dutton's flat, for there was no other sitting-room. She could not hang about the street, waiting for him to depart, it was far too cold. There was no alternative. She must go up to Simon Ewing's empty apartment.

Reluctant as she was, the slight shock of realizing the inspector's proximity so unexpectedly drove her into action. With the passing thought that she hoped George would not be late, for she did not really like the idea of being alone in that flat, she quickly mounted the stairs, opened the top door with the key, and entering the flat, walked towards the drawing-room door. She pushed it open, and then came to a sudden stop, transfixed by what she saw. For the flat was not empty after all.

Inspector Woods had suffered a check. Investigations had been made, and, to Woods's bitter disappointment, showed that George Fordham could not have been the watcher in the street. Dr. Ainslie had said he saw the man at 4.30. He had been on his way to visit a patient in the next-door block of flats. Inquiries had confirmed the fact that the doctor arrived there at the time stated.

Now, it had been found that at 4.30 George Fordham had rung up a business friend from a call box. The friend was a perfectly respectable and reliable person, who was quite positive that George had spoken to him at the hour named. It had been fixed by the fact that he had been on the point of making a trunk call to Scotland himself, and had done so immediately George rang off. The telephone authorities corroborated these times, but as the call had come through from the public telephone box without any hitch, there was no indication from which call box it had come.

As to why George had used a call box, it was proved that his own office line had been out of order; he had reported it to the authorities. The fault had been found to be in the instrument in the office, and had been dealt with the next day.

Brought to a standstill in this direction, Woods had determined to pay one final visit to Clevedon Street. The premises were now to be given up officially by the police. The Kensington Museum had sealed up the cabinets containing the collections. Everything had been swept and garnished. The police photographs were all filed away in the office, the record of the fingerprints accompanying them. Again and again those files had been studied. Nothing ever emerged from them. Now George Fordham was to take possession. Soon the flat would be cleared, and if possible let. Woods could not resist paying one final visit, but as he came down the stone staircase to the front door he realized that he must give up. From the flat itself no proof could be obtained of the facts Woods sought to establish.

Now he hesitated, as he stood under the portico. Vaguely his mind recurred to the Wallace case. *Could* his time-table be wrong? No, it had been checked again and again. Yet he felt dissatisfied. He wondered if Mrs. Dutton were at home. If so, there were one or two little points she might clear up for him. He rang at the bell. She was at home, and came to let him in herself.

At the sight of her visitor a slight look of dismay crossed her face, but she said nothing, and led the way to her sitting-room. Anne Godfrey was seated there, and she too looked up with an air which almost bordered on hostility.

Woods had long since learnt, however, that though officially the police are the protectors and benefactors of the law-abiding, yet, in practice, all human beings—even those with no sort of stain on their character, with no suspicion of anything secret or wrong in their lives—feel constraint, if not alarm, when a policeman appears at their door.

Not allowing himself, therefore, to be in any way affected by the manifest lack of pleasure at his appearance, he took the seat offered him, glancing as he did so at the clock on the mantelpiece to see how much time he could allow for this visit, and began as cheerfully and reassuringly as he could:

"I'm sure, Mrs. Dutton, you'll be glad we've taken off the man on duty upstairs. We hand over to-day to Mr. Ewing's representatives."

"Yes," said Mrs. Dutton, rather stiffly, "I must say I was glad when I heard he had gone. It is not very agreeable to have the police about. I only wish to forget everything to do with this dreadful affair as soon as possible. Indeed," as Woods made no reply, "I shouldn't care to stay on here another day now, if it were not that I could hardly hope to find a good tenant in the circumstances."

" And, after all, Aunt Mary," put in Anne pacifically, "we shall soon be off to Mentone. It's only for three or four weeks now."

"If you're going abroad, Mrs. Dutton," said Woods, seizing his opportunity, "I should just like to get clearly from you now one thing I had not pressed before, and which I want to make sure of."

Mrs. Dutton looked uneasy. She had hoped the process of interrogation was over for her. She had no alternative, however, but to say stiffly: "Anything I can tell you, Inspector, of course I will."

"On the evening of the murder," said Woods directly, "you were all sitting round this fireplace when the crash came overhead."

"Yes," agreed Mrs. Dutton.

"Now, when the fall came, up above, the time was about 5.15?"

"Yes," said Mrs. Dutton once more, marvelling at being taken over this old ground.

"Now, was that by your watch, or by this clock?"

Mrs. Dutton looked helplessly at Anne, who, however, gave her no help, but remained silent.

"I'm sure I can't say, Inspector," she said doubtfully. "When we spoke of it afterwards, we thought the time was between ten minutes past five and a quarter-past; but I don't know how we knew that. Do you remember, Anne?"

Anne, who had been staring at the inspector, recalled her attention to her aunt with a start.

"Oh! I think either Henry or I said it was at that time, Aunt Mary, and I think we went by the clock on the mantelpiece."

Woods looked rather grave. "Think again, please, Miss Godfrey. This really is an important point. We *must* fix the time of that fall correctly. Was the clock right that evening? I see it is slow now."

Anne made no reply, but Mrs. Dutton said uncertainly: "I really don't think I know for certain, Inspector. The clock doesn't keep very good time, but I can't say now if it was slow that day or not."

Woods went on patiently: "Can you think of anything you can fix the time by in another way? Miss Godfrey let her brother in, I understand?"

"Yes."

"And you came up from the basement?"

"Yes, I did. And now I remember I thought I heard the church clock strike just before I heard Henry arrive; and when I came up I did notice the clock on the mantelpiece didn't make it quite the hour."

Woods's expression brightened.

"Now, Mrs. Dutton, are you sure of that? This may alter our time-table, and, as I say, the exact and correct moment when you heard the fall is vital. I must try and fix it accurately."

"Yes," replied Mrs. Dutton, more definitely. "I really do remember that idea of our clock not being the same as the church chime coming into my head. I am sure of that."

"Very well," said Woods, fixing his clear, hard gaze on her, "I should like you just to write me out a brief statement of that."

He moved across to the writing-table, which stood at the far end of the room. He pulled out a chair for her, and she obediently sat down and prepared to write. Woods sat down beside her. Anne, thoroughly unhappy at this new development, hovered near.

Thus all of them were at the far side of the room, Woods and Mrs. Dutton with their backs to the windows, Anne looking towards them. None of them were in a position to see the street. Sound, however, could reach them clearly through the open window, and thus it was that Woods, as Mrs. Dutton paused in the act of beginning to write, distinctly heard a door slam. He listened a moment, then turned swiftly on Mrs. Dutton.

"That was a front door. Was it yours, Mrs. Dutton? No one seems to be coming in; was it someone going out?"

"No," replied that lady, startled and surprised. "There is no one here but Anne and myself."

Woods jumped up and hurried across the room, glancing out of the window as he rushed to the door. He was out, and on the steps, with extraordinary swiftness, but no one was in sight. He hesitated for a moment, then turned back.

"Miss Godfrey," he said, addressing Anne earnestly, "did you hear a door slam?"

"Yes," said Anne, the colour leaving her face. "I heard it, and I thought it sounded like the flat next door—Mr. Ewing's flat."

At this confirmation of his own suspicions, Woods wasted no more time. He pulled from his pocket the keys which he had still retained. He ran across to the next door, opened it, and the two women, still standing on their own threshold, heard his feet go rushing up the stairs.

Chapter XIII

THE ARTIST

And in a breath, bidden retell his tale.

Tertium Quid, R. BROWNING.

Meanwhile, in the row of buildings opposite, Riley was patiently conducting a house-to-house inquiry, trying to obtain any further information or corroboration of Dr. Ainslie's story as to the unknown watcher.

He had just arrived at Hetherington's flat, and was with great difficulty extracting information, piece by piece, from that gentleman.

Hetherington's tall, well-set-up figure lounged against the mantelpiece, and with careless indifference he listened to Riley's request for information. The sergeant could hardly believe this to be anything but a pose; it seemed to him incredible that anyone, living opposite to the scene of a murder, should take so little interest.

The artist, however, assured him that he "cared for none of these things." He was completely vague as to anything which had happened during the past week, and Riley began to find it almost impossible to pin him down to any definite facts.

"You admit a man came to your door that night, sir?"

"Yes, but I keep on telling you he wasn't anyone I knew. I didn't recognize him then, and I've never seen him since."

"Quite so, sir. Now, can you tell me what the time was when he rang your bell?"

"Oh! Between four and five o'clock."

"Can't you put it nearer than that, sir? A lot turns on the time, you know."

"Well," said Hetherington meditatively, "I'd had a man in to put up some shelves and so on. He knocked off soon after four, as he said he'd to go to another job. I tidied things up a bit, and had a smoke and so on, and then, just when I was starting a piece of work, this chap came and rang. I didn't look at the time."

"Can you fix it the other way about, sir? Did anything happen to make you notice the time after he'd gone?"

"Well, now you bring something back to me. I remember, directly after he'd gone, I went back to my easel, and as I picked up my bit of charcoal the clock at the church behind there struck five."

"Come," said Riley cheerfully, "that does help us. He must have been up here, then, at about five minutes to five?"

"Yes," nodded Hetherington, "I'll agree to that."

"Then, sir, how long was it after that you were fetched across to Mrs. Dutton's?"

"I wasn't fetched," said Hetherington perversely.

"Then how did you come to go across?"

"Well, I heard a woman screaming, and I looked out, and I saw a sort of commotion going on in the porch over there, and then someone being pulled and helped in from the front steps to the flat which I now know was Mrs. Dutton's. Then I saw someone come rushing out and go flying across to the doctor's and begin hammering and knocking like mad. So I thought I'd stroll out and see whatever was wrong."

"H'm. When you heard what was wrong, didn't you think about this man at your door?"

"No. Why should I? He looked a perfectly ordinary sort of fellow, and really it didn't seem to me a matter of any importance at all.

I forgot clean about him, and as I told you before, I don't think I've given him a thought from the moment I saw him until you turned up this afternoon."

"But, if you'll excuse me, sir, didn't it ever once occur to you that you had a man here, inquiring for a person who didn't and never had lived in your flat, roughly at the very time when it was known the murder opposite was committed?"

"No, it did not," replied the artist calmly. "I don't pay attention to all the Tom-fools who come knocking at my door. As far as I know, a fellow called Finlay might have been here before me."

"Can you describe your visitor?" But long experience had made the sergeant sceptical as to any helpful answer to this inquiry.

"Well, I don't know that I can. I just saw him for a moment. Didn't want to stay chatting with him."

" You're an artist, sir," said Riley craftily. "I'd expect you to notice more than another. Didn't you notice his build or his colouring at all? Just something, perhaps, you can call to mind?"

Slightly gratified by this small tribute, Hetherington was preparing to give more consideration to the matter than he had hitherto vouchsafed.

"Well—" he began, but for the present he got no further. The telephone bell rang, loudly and insistently. Hetherington took up the receiver, but turned at once to Riley.

"It's for you, Sergeant. Inspector Woods wants you."

Riley, greatly surprised, picked up the receiver and heard Woods's tones, full of unmistakable agitation, though he was striving to keep his tones level.

"That you, Riley? I saw you go in to Mr. Hetherington's and I thought I'd catch you. Come across at once to Mr. Ewing's flat. I'm there. Urgent." Riley could hear the receiver slammed down, and perceiving that no time must be lost, he barely stopped to say a word to Hetherington, and dashed at once down the steps and across the street.

There Anne Godfrey met him, her face positively ghastly. She pointed up to the staircase of flat B. "Up there, Sergeant, at once. There's been another murder. Young Mrs. Fordham this time!"

Completely taken aback, Riley was up the stairs as hard as he could pelt. The door of the flat stood open. Rushing in, he heard Woods call him from the drawing-room. Entering it, he could at first see no one. Then the inspector raised himself into view from behind the door, where he had been kneeling.

"We're too late, Riley, look here!"

Riley looked. Against the wall, sheltered from the door by the big lacquer screen, stood a large chesterfield sofa. It had originally been filled with cushions at either end. Some of them lay scattered on the floor; one had been thrown aside to the middle of the room, apparently by Woods himself.

Lying on the sofa, huddled up, her clothes disordered, her hands clenched, was the body of Penelope Fordham. Her bright, pale, golden hair scattered over a cushion made identification easier than would have been possible had the judgment to be formed solely from her congested face.

"How was it done, sir?"

"Suffocated! Held down, and the cushion pressed on her face," returned Woods briefly.

"How long ago?" began Riley, but Woods interrupted him. "Not long. She's still warm, of course. But actually I was up here myself not much more than half an hour ago."

At this very moment the sound of steps was heard coming up the stairs outside, and rounding the corner whence the front door of the flat could be seen.

"Nell! Nell! Are you there?" called a man's voice.

Woods rose hastily to his feet and moved towards the door.

"Her husband!" he exclaimed. "Riley, just stand between him and the body a moment."

As he spoke he intercepted George Fordham in the very act of entering the room.

"I'm sorry, Mr. Fordham," he said authoritatively," you can't come in here for the moment."

"Not come in?" said George, astonished and angry. "Why, what are you doing here? I thought you'd given up your occupation of this flat, Inspector. I understood it was permissible now for me to come and arrange about the furniture. I'm meeting my wife here at 4 o'clock. It's just on that now."

All this time he and Woods had faced each other in the lobby, George apparently determined to come in, Woods blocking his way.

"Sorry, sir. Something has occurred. I must ask you to wait."

Just then fresh footsteps were heard hastening upwards, and two more uniformed men made their appearance. Woods beckoned to one.

"Show Mr. Fordham into the back bedroom here, Curtis, and you, Roberts," turning to the other one, "stand at this door and see that no one comes in. *No one*, do you hear?"

He stepped back swiftly and shut the door in the faces of the little group outside.

Turning again to Riley, who was now kneeling down and peering into the disfigured and scarcely recognizable face," See here, Riley," and he pointed to the clenched hand hanging over the side of the sofa, adding hastily: "Don't touch her, though."

Riley looked carefully. The fingers of the right hand were clasped together. Something glittered from between them. Very cautiously Woods began to poke at the hand with a penholder he snatched up from the bureau. In a moment or two he had, without moving the position of the fingers, brought what lay within the palm into view. An irrepressible exclamation burst from Riley.

"Good God Almighty! The missing rings!"

For a moment Woods stood silent. He looked first at the limp body, then at the outflung hand with just the gleam and glitter of the stones showing within it. Then, with a sigh, he sat down in one of the chairs and buried his face in his hands.

"I was here an hour ago, Riley. I looked in to see everything had been left tidy and in good order. I only left half an hour since. I called in below to see if Mrs. Dutton was at home. I don't suppose I was talking to her for more than ten minutes. This wouldn't have happened if I'd stayed up here another quarter of an hour."

Riley stood appalled. He felt completely at sea.

"Why has it been done?" he said stupidly, for he knew Woods could not answer him. "No one could be in here to steal—and, as we know, there was no clue for anyone to want to remove," he added more slowly.

Woods raised his head.

"You mean, you're thinking that perhaps she was involved in the first murder?"

"Yes, she might have been mixed up in that, and come up here to-day, knowing we'd gone. Come to fetch something or put something right maybe—or else to meet her accomplice, that mysterious man—they quarrelled over these rings, all they'd got out of the murder, and he wanted to silence her."

He stopped, and then went on rather heavily, as if reluctant to voice his thoughts with the body, still warm, lying before him:

"Things look very queer to me. There are these rings in her hand. We know the murderer took them from Mr. Ewing. We know she had the third one in her possession, and didn't produce it until she thought you were on to her. This girl here was the last person to see the old man alive, though she tried to conceal that fact too. And she knew of the existence of the jewels." He spoke more quickly as link by link seemed to forge itself before him. "We don't really know that she ever left here at five o'clock that day at all. We've been assuming the robbery and murder was the work of the man, and we've never discovered for certain how he got in. Suppose the old man never let him in at all, but that this girl waited there and opened the door to him? He might have gone up to do the robbery while she undertook to keep old Ewing quiet?"

He hesitated a moment, trying to see how it all fitted. Woods did not interrupt but stared at him thoughtfully.

"That all fits in, sir, and it would account for the man being upstairs and being caught. He'd not have known, probably, what was going on in the drawing-room. He'd think she'd answer the bell, and never bother until he heard those other two, Godfrey and the Nurse, actually coming into the flat. That's why he wasn't blood-stained at all, I'll be bound."

"Do you think, then, she did the murder?" queried Woods curtly.

Riley glanced down at the body.

"Well, one wouldn't have thought it possible. Yet, you know, women *have* killed others by violence—just think of that maidservant who did in her mistress and chopped her all up. Don't you think it might be her very lack of strength which produced the great number of blows? She *could* have done it, seems to me."

Woods shook his head wearily. "No, I can't agree with you. I think that man wasn't stained because he'd stood up and had the seat of the chair between him and the body. I think in that way he was protected from spurts and splashes, and he'd keep his hands clean. You've nothing here to incriminate this girl."

"Except the rings," interjected Riley. "Surely they're conclusive?"

"Conclusive, yes, but not of her guilt." He pointed down at the hand once more." Stoop down and see for yourself. Look closely and you'll see they're lying in her palm quite loosely. Dead hands don't relax, you know. If she'd held them tightly before death, they'd be tightly held still. But that isn't so. Her hand really isn't clasped on them at all. They're lying perfectly loose."

"You mean, the hand has been closed round them——?"

"After death," finished Woods. "The rings were pushed inside her hand after she'd been smothered, but the hand, though it was pressed close round them, didn't grip—couldn't, of course. So there they lie as evidence, to me at any rate, of her innocence and of someone else's efforts to incriminate her."

"But," expostulated Riley, not completely convinced, "even if that is so, it still doesn't prove her free of the other murder. To my mind, if she were guilty of that it all fits together, and she might quite well have come here to meet that man. On my theory she and he were accomplices. She'd got those rings, all they *did* get out of Mr. Ewing's death as it happened, and they met here to settle what they'd do. It would be a good place, as no one else was likely to come here, and she had a right. Indeed"——pointing to a ring with a little bundle of keys on it which lay on the table—"she'd got the keys, you see, to let herself in. Then supposing she and he quarrelled over them, and he went too far and then wanted to silence her, he'd leave the rings behind and so get rid of an incriminating bit of evidence."

"No," retorted Woods. "You don't change my opinion. I don't read the story of those rings like that. If she'd stolen them, and they'd quarrelled over them, she'd have been clutching them tight, you may be sure of that. That isn't so at all. You've got to think of another explanation to fit the facts. My own idea is that she's had nothing to do with the crime."

For the moment Riley was silent. Then he moved away from the body and began to glance keenly about the room, seeking any signs of something untoward. He began methodically to inspect all the cabinets in particular, taking in the appearance of the tapes and seals, all of which were unbroken and quite in order. "None of these cabinets has been opened. The bureau's empty, just as we left it. Nothing seems to have been touched."

"Yes, but this cabinet isn't as we left it," said Woods, excitedly moving away from the sofa, for his eye had been caught by a very minute heap of white dust at the base of the one to the right of the fireplace.

"I'll swear that dust wasn't there when I was here a while back. It catches the eye against the black of the lacquer."

Both men stooped, but there seemed at first nothing much to see. The tiny little heap of dust was apparently the scrapings of a small gash or jag made in the lacquer itself, running along the bottom edge of the cabinet at the side towards the ground, just where the wood touched the painted wall. There was nothing else, the small jagged tear on the surface of the cabinet, the powder lying on the ground.

Riley merely looked, considering whether the museum's officials had made this scratch when they sealed up the collection. Woods, however, went down, and tried to push his finger in behind. He failed, however, the space was too small. Drawing a stout knife from his pocket he opened it, and tried to prise this in behind. This too failed, but the knife slipping, inflicted a fresh wound on the polished side of the cabinet. The black lacquer flaked away and fell in powder. With a grim little nod Woods returned the knife to his pocket, as though well satisfied. He then began to scrutinize closely the keyhole and sealed tapes securing the door of the cabinet.

"Just come and look, Riley. Do you think anyone has been tampering with this?"

Riley in his turn bent to look. "Well, I do think so." He touched one of the seals very gingerly; it moved and the tape which it secured sagged. "Yes, you see, someone has put a heated blade behind it. They've meant to open this door."

The two scrutinized the lock, but it showed no signs of having been turned.

"I think," said Woods, "whoever it was got the wax seal loose, but got no further. We must send for the museum's people, of course, to make sure nothing's gone from the cabinet, but I think myself they'll find nothing is missing."

At this moment a louder sound of angry voices swelled up from the next room. Riley nodded his head in that direction. "That's her husband, giving trouble. I expect he's getting restless; he must guess there's something badly wrong."

"Yes, and of course he said he was to meet her here; probably he's wondering at her non-appearance."

"What'll you say to him?"

Woods stared down at the limp, contorted body. "He'll have to be allowed to come in. Well, I'll get it over at once," he said briefly, and turned towards the door.

Woods and Riley stood together once more in the empty drawing-room. The usual paraphernalia had been brought. Photographs had been taken, fingerprints looked for. Now all was done, and Penelope's body had been taken away.

Riley glanced at his superior. Woods was very pale, but there was a faint atmosphere of confidence about him which communicated itself to Riley, slightly strung up as he was by the scene they had just passed through.

George Fordham had behaved like a madman. Thoroughly infuriated by the inspector's earlier refusal to allow him to enter the drawing-room, he had stormed and sworn, and even when told of the death of his wife had scarcely appeared to take in the news, so furious was his temper. When at length Woods, calm and persistent, had succeeded in forcing him to give his attention to the police, he turned sullen, and was extremely unwilling to give them any information or help.

He merely reiterated that he had come to meet his wife at 4 o'clock, that she had the keys in her possession, that she had, as far as he knew, come on from her dentist, and that he had arrived a little behind his time, to find the police in possession. He knew nothing, of course, of the rings, and seemed to have been rendered quite stupid by the shock and excitement.

He had therefore been allowed to go home. A plainclothes man accompanied him in order to search Penelope's papers, in case any clue might be discovered amongst them. Efforts had now to be made to trace Penelope's movements that afternoon.

"You see, Riley," said Woods, "this second murder is going to help us to solve the first. The same man has done both. I don't think this was premeditated; I think Mrs. Fordham turned up here before she was expected. She surprised someone here. I'm pretty well certain I know who it was, and why he was here. I'm pretty well certain, too, that he's really done for himself now. I believe he's given me the very piece of evidence I've been after all this while. But I've a few details to be checked and fitted in before I go for an arrest. I want to take a risk too—try a piece of bluff which may help me a great deal. If the man I suspect is after all innocent, he'll not fall into the trap. If he's guilty—well, I'll catch him with it." A fierce, angry note crept into his voice as he said these words. Aware of the sound himself, he looked at Riley, and for once his clear blue eyes seemed to blaze. Riley was fascinated, for, well as he knew Woods, he had never before seen him stirred in just this way.

"Why," said Woods, still speaking with that fierce undertone of violence, "I'd risk anything, pretty well do anything, to catch this fellow. He's beyond the pale. A man who's used his strength to kill first an old man, a cripple, then a woman—and tried to use his brains to fasten the guilt on her—" He broke off, and then added more calmly: "Well, I shall always blame myself I wasn't up here to prevent this second crime. I might have foreseen what he'd be up to, but I didn't foresee her presence at the time—nor could I have done so, I think. But there's this one gleam of consolation. We were so close at hand, and the murderer must have seen your car across the road, he must have feared we might come up, and so he got rattled. He overlooked one all-important detail, or I hope he did, and that will just suffice to hang him."

Chapter XIV

THE END

The deed maladroit yields three deaths instead of one.

The Other Half-Rome, R. BROWNING.

H e ended, having recovered his calm, and resuming his usual rather quiet business-like manner, turned back to Riley.

"There's nothing for us to do here now, or rather nothing for me. You take charge here, and I'll be off and get on with my inquiries."

He went out of the flat and down the stairs. As he went out of the front door into the street Mrs. Dutton, who had clearly been waiting for him, came out of her flat.

"Inspector, could you spare just one moment?"

Glancing at her white face and shaking hands, and understanding what the shock to this woman must be, and genuinely sorry for her, Woods nodded.

"I've just a moment, Mrs. Dutton, but try not to keep me. There are things I must be getting on with." He stepped inside her door and stood with her in the passage.

"Yes, of course," replied the poor lady, very unsteadily. "I'm sorry to disturb you. But my niece and I simply can't stay here, we both feel that. We want to go away now, at once. Have you any objection? I mean, I know you'll want to ask us about Penelope, about her arrangements to come here and so on, but if we just go to a hotel somewhere in town will that be all right?"

Woods paused and reflected. He saw that this proposed arrangement might fit in very well with his plans, but it was rather difficult for him to decide on the spur of the moment what he wished done. Eventually he made up his mind.

"Well, Mrs. Dutton, I quite understand your feelings, and as long as I know where you are, and how I can get at you, you are perfectly at liberty to go where you like. If you go to a hotel, or friends, please let us know at once, and please be sure you are on the telephone."

Seeing the involuntary look of fear which crossed her face, he added very gravely: "I needn't tell you this is a terribly serious matter, Mrs. Dutton. And I do tell you, in confidence, that I think I am going to solve the problems of these murders, but I'm afraid it's going to be a bad business, and time mustn't be wasted. There mustn't be any delay at any point. Will your niece be with you, do you think?"

"I don't know," she answered; "it rather depends on whether we go to friends or not. If we go to friends, I expect we should separate, but if we don't find anyone who can take us in at such short notice, then we shall keep together and go to a hotel. I couldn't be by myself," she added, with a violent and irrepressible shudder.

A thought struck Woods. "Just one thing, Mrs. Dutton. You were at home all this afternoon, I understand?"

"Yes, I was."

"In which room were you between three and four o'clock?"

"I was resting in my own bedroom, until you came to see me."

" Your room looks out on the back?"

"Yes."

"So you can't tell me when Mrs. Fordham went up to the flat?"

Mrs. Dutton looked ready to faint. "No, indeed I can't, Inspector. I wasn't in this room by myself at all, the whole afternoon."

"Your niece, where was she?"

" She was downstairs in her own room until you called; that was at about half-past three, so she told me."

"Then no one was in this sitting-room during the afternoon from three o'clock to four, except when we three were here together?"

"No one."

"And this is the only room that gives a view of the front steps?" queried Woods.

Mrs. Dutton nodded. "Yes; actually the spare-room, which my niece has been using, looks on to the street, but the portico sticks out, and one can't see that part of the steps which leads to the upper flat from her window."

Woods noted this fact, and then went on more briskly: "Well, I just wanted to be quite sure, Mrs. Dutton; now I must be off. Please ring up the station directly you've fixed on where you're going," and without further delay he returned to his office.

There an hour later Brown came in to report on the result of his search amongst the papers in Penelope's desk and drawers.

"I don't know that I found anything of importance, sir," he said. "There were a lot of household bills and things, mostly paid. I'd say from what I found they were living very much on the poverty line. I've brought along her household accounts, and you'll see for yourself how small they are."

"Any personal accounts?"

"Hardly any. She must have paid cash mostly. Just a few receipted bills, nothing outstanding that I could find. I did notice one odd thing, though, and brought it along."

He produced a business order book. It had a plain cloth cover, and within a block of bill-heads, stamped with the office address of a floor-covering firm. About half had been used, and only the perforated counterfoils remained.

"This was pushed in amongst some other things in her drawers, sir. It clearly isn't hers, and I imagine is her husband's."

"Why did you bring it?"

"Well, sir," with some hesitation, "I thought in a case like this anything at all out of the ordinary ought to be reported. Of course it probably got in there by mistake; she may have picked it up with some other books and papers and just crammed it in. But actually I brought it along because I noticed one odd thing about it."

He laid the little book open and pushed it towards Woods, who bent forward to look at the blank top page.

"Of course this page on the top hasn't been used, sir, but you can see in a good light the impressions and cracks left by the entry on the last page. They were done with a deep pencil or pen and they've marked through."

Woods carried the book to the window, and sloping it to the right could see Brown's statement was correct. He could make out a few words, quite clearly dented upon the blank page.

"Can you read anything, sir?" said Brown anxiously.

"Yes, I can see part of an address. Printed in block capitals. Something ending in 'iggton', and below that 52 Ber St., N.W."

"Yes, sir," triumphantly, "that's what I thought. And, you see, I happen to know Ber Street myself, and I know there's no one living at 52 with a name ending in 'iggton'."

Woods stared.

"What's that you say?"

"Well, I happen to come from Norwich, sir, and Ber Street is one of the old streets there, and so it took my attention when I came to London and was studying up the maps. I noticed a Ber Street up in the north-west, and I happened to be up that way one free afternoon, and just for curiosity I looked it up and walked along it. It's only a very short street, a cul-de-sac, and there's no 52 in it."

"Sure of that?"

"Quite sure, sir, all the more so because our Ber Street at home is a great big wide place; they say it's an old Roman road in fact, so I took all the more notice of this one being so small."

"Go up there now and make an official report, Brown. And send for Frinton; we'll have to get this book tested and the marks photographed. Glad you brought it along."

With a smile of congratulation he turned back to his desk, and Brown hurried off to do his congenial errand.

At ten o'clock the next morning Mrs. Dutton was awoken from an uneasy sleep by the sound of the telephone trilling outside her door. She had been taken in by some friends, but their small house had only one spare-room. In consequence Anne had been obliged to inflict herself on Henry and Doreen. She had professed not to share her aunt's nervousness, and had wished to go to a hotel by herself, declaring peace and solitude were what she personally needed, but her aunt's horror at the idea had prevailed upon her to go to her brother. Solitude was actually the last thing Mrs. Dutton desired, and the violence with which her heart began to beat at the sound of the telephone made her feel quite ill. Almost immediately the door opened, and the maid appeared.

"I'm sorry to disturb you, madam, but it's the police inspector."

"Oh! Does he want to speak to me?" in a trembling voice.

"No, madam, I told him you were still in bed, and he said a message would do. He wants to know if he may use your flat this morning? He says, to tell you he wants to see Mr. George Fordham and one or two other people there, if you have no objection?"

"Oh yes," answered Mrs. Dutton, rather mystified, but thankful nothing more was required of her. "Tell him of course he can. I left the keys with the porter at the residential hotel."

In another moment or two the maid returned.

"He says to thank you, madam, and he is arranging to see Mr. Fordham there this morning, and he'll tell the porter to let Mr. Fordham have the key if he gets there first."

Mrs. Dutton felt too tired to take much interest in the inspector's arrangements, and sank off into a doze again.

She was dimly aware that a little later the telephone rang again, but no one came to disturb her. When the maid brought her belated breakfast in she said:

"I didn't disturb you again, madam; Mr. Godfrey said I'd better not. He rang up to know if you could tell him where Mr. Fordham was likely to be this morning. So I told him what the inspector had arranged, and he said that was what he wanted to know and rang off."

Thankful she was only required to listen and acquiesce and that no active effort was demanded of her, Mrs. Dutton peacefully began upon her toast and coffee.

No such peace and content were to be found in the flat she had deserted. There Woods and Riley were foregathered in the front sitting-room, waiting in an anxiety which was proclaimed by their movements. Woods kept glancing at the clock.

"It's going to turn on the time, Riley," he broke out, as the clock chimed eleven o'clock. "You're sure you told Fordham not to be later than eleven?"

" Quite sure," replied Riley. "I told him you must see him at once, and here, and you'd be gone yourself before a quarter-past eleven."

"And you told the Godfreys that Mr. Fordham wanted to see Mr. Godfrey, most urgently?"

"Yes, I carried out your instructions quite accurately. Asked to speak to Miss Godfrey, then told her it was a mistake, I'd wanted Mr. Godfrey, but gave her the message, and rang off at once."

"Well," said Woods, "that's quite right, that's all we can do. We must just hope for the best now—ah! here he is!"

As he spoke he had been looking out of the window, and had beheld George Fordham's figure coming along the opposite side of the road. To Riley's surprise, Fordham, instead of coming across to No. 5, turned in at the door opposite, and hastened rapidly up the steps and out of sight.

"Why, where on earth has he gone?" he asked aloud.

"Well, I got Hetherington to send him a line, saying he must see him, and at once. I fancy he's just gone up there now to see what's up, before keeping his appointment with me."

They stood waiting a few minutes, but almost immediately George reappeared, this time accompanied by Hetherington, who came striding across the street, side by side with the slimmer and rather taller figure of Fordham.

"Go and let them in, Riley," said Woods, "but I'll go into the back room. Bring Mr. Fordham in here and send Mr. Hetherington in to me in Mrs. Dutton's bedroom. Don't tell them I'm there. Be quick."

Indeed George's violent ring at the front door was already being followed up by an impatient tattoo on the knocker.

Riley hastened along the passage, while Woods slipped quickly into the back bedroom. From there he heard Riley's voice.

"Good morning, Mr. Fordham, the inspector wants you to wait in the sitting-room if you don't mind. He'll be with you in a moment."

"What on earth is he up to?" snapped George in reply. "What does the fellow want, I'd like to know? First he rings me up at my house and says he wants to see me here. Why on earth here? This isn't his house, it's Mrs. Dutton's. And then I get a message from Mr. Hetherington that he must see me at once. I go in there and find the inspector's been leaving messages with him to bring me across here. What's it all about? I'm not going to put up with this mystery and nonsense, I can tell you! What's the fellow up to, I say?"

"You'd better ask the inspector that yourself, sir," said Riley pacifically, as he shepherded George into the front room. "Mr. Hetherington, I'd just like a word with you."

George turned to glare angrily, but Riley swiftly shut the door upon him, stepped outside, and actually stood prepared to prevent his coming out into the passage, as a brief glimpse of his angry, lowering face had almost threatened.

At this juncture Woods appeared at the door of the back room.

"Well, Mr. Hetherington," he said softly and anxiously. "What do you say."

Hetherington looked at him for the fraction of a moment in silence, and then said quite firmly: "That's not the man who came to my door that night, Inspector. I'm quite sure. This fellow has a different build, and he didn't stand in the same way, and his voice wasn't the same. I'm really quite positive it's not the same man."

Riley looked if possible even blanker and more surprised than before as his gaze went to Woods's face. For the inspector, instead of being surprised or cast down by Hetherington's statement, appeared quite satisfied and almost pleased.

"Well, Mr. Hetherington, that's what I really was expecting you to say. I didn't think this was the same man, but I wanted confirmation of my idea if I could get it. Your impression has made me feel what I'm going to do is right."

At this moment a rat-tat-tat came at the door below. Woods glanced at his watch, noticed it was just on the quarter-past, and, going softly to the head of the stairs leading down to the basement, gave a very low whistle. In response to this a couple of shadowy figures began to emerge from the unlit quarters below. As they reached the top of the staircase they were revealed as uniformed constables, and behind them appeared to be more still.

Glancing into Hetherington's amazed face, Woods silently indicated the front door.

"Don't wait, Mr. Hetherington, get back to your own flat. I'm afraid this isn't going to be the place for any of the public."

Rather reluctantly Hetherington obeyed, and started for the door. He noticed that Riley, following behind him, did not latch it, and looking back as he crossed the road, he saw that in fact it was set slightly but distinctly ajar.

Meanwhile, having seen Hetherington off the premises, the sergeant obeyed Woods's beckoning finger, and, followed by two of the uniformed men, they advanced into the drawing-room.

George, who had been standing in the window, turned his furious red face upon them. He was clearly prepared to burst out into a volley of abuse when Woods, going forward with a hand outstretched towards him, touched him on the shoulder and said in a voice which sounded unnaturally loud in the silence that had fallen: "George Fordham, I arrest you in the name of the law for the murder of your wife."

The next moment pandemonium broke forth. Fordham leapt straight at the inspector, his hands striking wildly and violently. Woods, shielding his face and throat, staggered. Riley rushed to the rescue, and Roberts flung himself on Fordham from behind. They crashed to the floor in a struggling heap.

Flying feet came tearing up the steps and along the passage, and Henry Godfrey suddenly appeared, dashing in from the street as the sound of tumult broke out. He stopped short on the threshold, petrified at the scene which met his eyes. Then, as he stood for a moment, the figure of Woods disentangled itself from the heap. Riley and Roberts between them held down an unrecognizable form, while the inspector, breathless and panting, bent to snap handcuffs on the wrists now held together by Riley.

Godfrey uttered no word. He only gazed until the two officers rose, dragging Fordham to stand upon his feet. Staring, still silent, into that convulsed face, Godfrey fell back a pace. While Woods and the others paused a moment, wiping their foreheads and recovering their composure, his hand went swiftly to his pocket. Before any of them had time to check him his hand rose to his mouth, a loud report, a cloud of smoke, and his body toppled over to lie in a crumpled heap.

"Curse it all," roared Woods savagely, "don't say that fellow has cheated the gallows!"

Chapter XV

THE FIRST SOLUTION

Being incomplete, my act escaped success.

Guido, R. BROWNING.

"Well, Inspector," said Hetherington, kicking the fire to an even brighter blaze, "come along in and sit down, and tell me all about it. Personally I feel I've assisted the course of justice and I've earned my reward."

As he spoke, the door opened and Dr. Ainslie came in. Seeing Woods, who had sunk with an air of fatigue into one of the big, shabby arm-chairs, struggling to rise to his feet, the doctor spoke hastily:

"Don't get up, Inspector. You look dead beat. Stay where you are, and Hetherington will give you something to buck you up. You've been on your feet all day, I know."

The kindliness with which the words were spoken made Woods feel here was a genuine effort to wipe out the unpleasantness of their last meeting. While Hetherington busied himself in getting glasses, a decanter, and a siphon out of a cupboard, Ainslie pulled up another chair, and Woods sank back comfortably, realizing with thankfulness that now at last he could relax. George Fordham had been removed, still shouting and swearing, to prison; Henry Godfrey had been removed, quite silent and still, to the mortuary. Woods, after his day's labours, had dropped in to assure Hetherington that the morning's manœuvres had not been meaningless. Now, at the close of a cold January day, he found himself very pleasantly established before a roaring fire, with a hospitable host ready to ply him with drink and tobacco, and, being a bachelor, with no home of his own to tempt him back, he was not unwilling to stay. But, while he might stay, he might not talk, in the sense of revealing what must wait for a trial to bring to light.

"No, sir," he said, turning to his host, "I'll stay and just have a chat, if I may, but I can't tell you anything about the case yet. But I promise you," seeing the look of disappointment in Hetherington's face, "I'll come back here one day, when the trial's been held, and I'll explain to you then what I've been after all these days."

Realizing the need for accepting this offer, Hetherington said no more, and, after a cheerful half-hour, Woods got up to go.

"I'm very grateful to you, Mr. Hetherington, and to you too, Doctor," turning to Ainslie, "for making me welcome and letting me have this rest. I dare say you can guess partly what a strain this case has involved. There's always a feeling of reaction once the man is caught. This has been worse than others," he added, a shade darkening his face, "because Mrs. Fordham oughtn't to have lost her life. No one could foresee what happened, and, of course, in my profession, as in others, one learns to put the past behind and just think of what one has to do in the present, but it's difficult for me to forget, though many people think a policeman has neither nerves nor imagination. It's been the greatest relief to me to have this restful evening, and I'll make some return for it later on, you may be sure."

He was gone before either of the two men had quite known what to say.

"H'm, yes," said the doctor, "I expect he does feel a reaction to-night, and he's still got the trial ahead of him. That's an anxiety, however sure of his ground he is."

Hetherington walked to the windows and gazed across the street. No lights shone from either No. 5A or B.

"Odd," he said, "to think how commonplace this street seemed when I moved in, less than a month ago. I used to look across and see those flats opposite lighted up. I watched the people in them one late afternoon while I waited for the furniture men. They seemed such ordinary, peaceable, middle-class people, prosperous, comfortable, friendly. Now those two homes are smashed up, and the flats won't be lived in for a long time, I should say. No one will be in a hurry to set up house in *those* rooms."

The doctor, who had come over to stand beside him, nodded agreement.

"No, can't say I should care to, myself. Well, I suppose it's all ended now. I shall look forward to hearing the inspector tell us how he brought it all about."

The two returned to the fireside, and the conversation turned to other topics.

Spring had almost come before Woods redeemed his promise, but the intervening months had not made him forgetful. One evening in early May he sat again in Hetherington's arm-chair. The doctor also, summoned by appointment, was installed opposite, and this time there was no need for Woods to observe professional secrecy.

"Well, Mr. Hetherington, if it will interest you and the doctor to know how I set about it, I'll tell you. The court proceedings only show you, so to speak, the climbers standing on the tops of the hills. Now I can tell you how we worked our way up. It takes endless patience to get the case together; I hope it won't require as much from you to listen to its reconstruction."

Hetherington laughed, and settled himself comfortably to listen. Dr. Ainslie said nothing, but merely lit his pipe.

"Now, this was the first situation I had to face. Mr. Simon Ewing was murdered, robbery being almost certainly the motive. No weapon was found, and the murderer left no scrap of his possessions behind.

If the man seen leaving were the murderer, he hadn't any traces on himself, so to speak, for his clothes weren't noticeably torn or stained, and he wasn't, as far as could be told, marked in any way. In short, we hadn't any definite clues.

"I solved the problem of the weapon as you heard in court. The old man was killed by blows from the leg of the chair. The murderer had swung it in his hands, and struck at the man on the floor, himself remaining upright, and thus inflicted the injuries from a fair distance. That is to say, his hands and arm did not come into close contact with his victim, nor was his face near enough to be splashed. Probably the chair, interposed between the two, kept off all stains. Certainly its under-surface was stained and not its upper. I saw that either the murderer was very far-seeing, and had decided beforehand to use something he found on the spot, or the crime wasn't premeditated, and he'd used what came nearest to his hand.

"From this two very important things followed. First, we must not expect the murderer to give us clues in the shape of blood-stained clothes. Second, the very use of this chair seemed to me to throw light on the personality of the murderer and his connexion with Simon Ewing.

"Now, in either case I felt there was some indication the murderer knew the flat and knew it well. I don't believe anyone, meaning to kill, would rely on the chance of there being a suitable weapon somewhere about; or if he'd only meant to rob, he must have thought he could get into the flat and take what he wanted without anyone preventing him. The way an entry could be effected did not puzzle me very much, once I saw the flat had an upper part with an empty room. Any visitor could, in certain circumstances, pretend to leave, and really go upstairs instead of out of the flat door. These circumstances would arise if Mr. Ewing were laid up with his rheumatism and if the nurse were out or down at a meal. In that case, anyone wanting to rob could get upstairs and let himself out again later without the old man hearing. Mr. Ewing was just recovering from a bad bout of his illness on the 20th, and though out of bed in the afternoon was confined to his sitting-room.

"I put this possible scheme of events against the knowledge that the jewellery had been, in fact, kept in that upstairs unused room. It seemed clear that the thing could have been done, but only by someone familiar with Mr. Ewing and who knew all these details—the geography of the house, the habits of Simon Ewing, and the existence of the jewellery.

"Anyone in possession of this information could plan a robbery. If anything went wrong, it would always be possible to render the old man helpless.

"Mind you, I deliberately don't put it more strongly than that, for I doubt if many men ever voice the idea of committing a murder to their inner selves. They don't go quite so far as to put these things even into the form of ideas; they leave them to the subconscious. It gives a sort of feeling of preserving the decencies, but I've no shadow of doubt the thought is lurking there underneath, and the man knows it, and knows he can call it forth and act upon it if the occasion should arise."

Woods paused and glanced at the doctor, who nodded briefly.

"Yes, I suppose that's sound psychology, Inspector. There are things George Fordham might not say to himself even if he thought them, though he'd have no scruples of any sort if action were needed."

Woods went on:

"Now, the next thing which struck me very forcibly, and which was indeed the outstanding feature in this crime, was the question of time, or, in other words, when was there the opportunity for someone to commit this murder? The nurse went out at 4 p.m. Mr. Ewing was left alone, but the murderer didn't go up until 5 o'clock, when the nurse, even if delayed, might reasonably have been expected back, since she was due to return no later than half-past four. I considered that the evidence of all the members of Mrs. Dutton's tea-party did definitely establish the fact that the murderer went up at 5 o'clock or just after, and that the murder took place when the heavy fall occurred at round about ten minutes past five.

"The murder *took place* then, but I wasn't convinced it was planned for that time. I was sure it had been intended to take place while the nurse was out. That was all I could feel was definite as to this question of opportunity, namely that the opportunity was provided between the hours of 4 and 5 p.m.

"Then I came on to the next stage. Given the opportunity, who would be likely to avail themselves of it? In other words, who had a motive? Or who, to narrow it a little further, amongst those persons familiar with the flat and with Mr. Ewing's habits?

"The first person to be considered was the nurse. She might have had all the knowledge required; she certainly knew of the opportunity, and either she herself or an accomplice might have taken it. It was, however, difficult to find a motive. Her character was investigated and was excellent. She was in no financial difficulty, and there seemed no adequate reason for her to be involved in the crime. Next came persons, not living in the flat, who knew Mr. Ewing well, and at once, heading the list, came George Fordham. He had knowledge of the flat, of his uncle's health, of his possessions, and he would have been readily admitted. Had he motive?

"We knew that he was very poor and in very low water. At first I could not get beyond that. In the very early stages of the investigation we had only suspicion to go on, and of course other people might be found who were equally implicated. We dared not be too open in our inquiries. The attempts I made to discover Fordham's financial position were not very successful; tentative questions at his place of business produced nothing. His employer had been an intimate friend of his parents, had taken George on out of kindness, and, not aware he was suspected of the murder, was trying to shield him from other investigations. We had no idea of this, and could make no progress in that direction.

"I think it will make things clearer, however, if I tell you now what I discovered later. The second murder put into my hands the very information I had sought in vain after the first. Through it I got proof of Fordham's career of fraud. As you know from the trial, the man sent to look through Mrs. Fordham's papers found the blank order book, with the impression left on the top page of a previous entry. We proved that entry was a false one. Fordham had been making use of false addresses. Armed with that, I then went back to his employer, and we soon unravelled the whole business.

"At first Fordham had begun quite honestly. He had obtained genuine orders for the firm, received payment for them, which he passed on, and claimed his due commission. Then, when he began to be pressed for money and in difficulties, he hit on an ingenious plan which, though dishonest in one sense, didn't at first involve stealing. He would book an order, and represent it as being for a smaller amount than it was, keeping for himself the difference in cash, which was greater than his commission would be. He would see that part of the order, corresponding to what he had reported as the total, was delivered, and he would notify the purchasing firm the rest was to follow. In biggish amounts of stuff like this, it often isn't all required at once, and it is quite usual for delivery to be made in instalments. He banked on that, of course. Later, when he'd got in fresh orders which enabled him to balance his cash, he'd send in the rest of the order and have it delivered. In this way his employer ultimately got the complete amount of business, Fordham got his commission, the buyer got his goods. Only during the interval Fordham had had control and use of part of the sum paid for the goods. His employer got wind of this, and, of course, Fordham, when found out, could not immediately produce all the money owing. Anxious not to send him to prison, his employer gave him notice that if restitution were made within a certain time, no prosecution would be made, he would simply be dismissed.

"What his employer did not know, and what that bill-book enabled us to discover, was, that his frauds had gone a step farther. Betting and speculation were the groundwork of his efforts to get straight, and in these hard times they had failed him. So he fell back on the crude expedient of booking up false orders for imaginary addresses. He never sent those false orders in to the warehouse, but up to the office where he claimed and received commission. He must have known this would come to light eventually, but he was a born gambler, always hoped he'd get the funds to replace his defalcations, and reckoned his employer would in that event be willing not to prosecute.

"When he knew he'd got to make good and somehow or other produce the money within six weeks—that was the time his employer allowed—he began to look round for any means whereby he could get the cash. He didn't tell either his wife or his uncle of his predicament. Instead, he invented this story of a possible partnership, and tried to induce old Ewing to advance him some money for it. If Simon had let him have this hundred or two, there would have been no robbery and no murder—or at least not at this stage. Whether George would have come to it at the end no one can tell. Judging from the savagery he showed since he gave rein to his worse nature, I think myself he'd have broken out sooner or later.

"However, all this story we only got in its entirety later. At the early stage, I considered Fordham a possible suspect. I believed his finances gave him a motive, and I set out to trace his associates and, of course, his movements on the day itself. First I wanted to know his whereabouts during the vital period Where was he at five o'clock? As you know, he hadn't tried for an absolute alibi, but that did him no harm. An innocent person might be hard put to it to produce an alibi, and that, of course, he knew. I did notice one small point. He'd told his wife he'd be back early that day, and it transpired that in point of fact he had not been early after all. That fitted with my theory. If the robbery or murder were originally planned for four o'clock, he *would* have been home early. As somehow it had been delayed for an hour, so he too had been delayed. Only theory, you'll say, but all these little straws showed the wind.

"Now, did this belief that a delay had occurred receive confirmation elsewhere? I believed that it did. For I thought I saw corroboration in the way in which the man was seen leaving the flat. He could never have intended that should happen; he must always have meant to get away before the nurse returned. She'd gone out, and met with the accident nearly an hour before. He couldn't have meant to stay so long. Of course, we had to bear in mind he'd never imagined, either, that she would return accompanied by anyone. He'd expect her to be alone, and he may have intended, if she should, by some mischance, arrive before he'd done, to silence her. He wouldn't, however, wish to do that unless it were absolutely forced upon him. He wouldn't want to let himself in for a double murder if he could avoid it. No, I was confident his plans had gone awry. He'd meant to have his job done as soon after four o'clock as possible, and be away. Now, if he'd been obliged to wait and go up to the flat at five o'clock instead of four, surely he'd have had to hang about outside? I began to hope that might be so, and to inquire if any such loiterer had been seen in the street. Unluckily for us, it had been cold and wet. People in that residential street were all at home, curtains drawn, no one either about or watching from the windows. No one came forward to make any report. Then I got on your tracks, Doctor, and you did at last tell me what I wanted."

He turned to Dr. Ainslie.

"Your evidence, when it came, caused me a lot of trouble, sir. I had begun to hope my way was to be made clear by your story of a watcher in the street. Instead, when I came to test and examine it, my trail became confused and split up. For the description you gave didn't tally with that of George Fordham. If you were speaking the truth, he was not the man hanging about in the street after all. Then you told me of Mr. Hetherington, and his description of the man who'd come to his flat tallied with yours. I had to reconsider my theory, and I'm bound to confess I had to look with an eye of suspicion upon you two. For neither of you had come forward to help the police; you'd both kept things to yourself, on your own showing. You were both newcomers to the neighbourhood, and, if you'll excuse me saying so, you were both found to be hard up."

He broke off at the rather rueful looks which dawned on the faces of his companions.

"Well, you know," he went on, "we have to find out these things, but, of course, they go no further, and I expect by now you know each other well enough for this to be no secret to either of you?"

Ainslie laughed.

"You're right there, Inspector, and, of course, Hetherington and I don't object in the least to you having the information. I only hope you also know we're both on the up-grade now."

"Well," said Woods, smilingly, "I'm glad to hear that, but, of course, three months ago your prospects weren't quite so good, and at least we had to consider you both as in need of cash. Then again, you lived so close to the scene of the crime, and had ample opportunity for watching it; in the case of both of you, your front windows overlooked the flats opposite; Dr. Ainslie knew Mr. Ewing, knew about the jewellery, knew, probably, when the nurse was out. There was quite a case piling up against you. What really made me not take you seriously"—this with again a slight smile at the doctor's horrified air—"was that question of time. I found you'd been seeing patients all the afternoon by appointment, and you'd gone in to Mrs. Fullard in these flats. You couldn't, of course, have managed the bicycle attack on Nurse Edwards. If you *had* been concerned, you'd have needed an accomplice. That was where Mr. Hetherington might have come in. He might have been in it with you. That wasn't really a serious proposition, but as I just sat turning things over in my mind, it came idly into my thoughts, as things do, and though I dismissed it in your case, for I didn't seriously suspect you, Doctor, it suddenly lit a train in my mind.

"Supposing this were a crime executed by two men after all, though not by you two, how would that theory fit the facts?

"Well, in that case we began to clear up one muddle. The watcher whom you two had described, it was clear, wasn't George Fordham, my chief suspect. If you told the truth, this person was shorter, more thick-set, fairish in colouring. Nor did this description tally with the one given by other people of the man seen leaving the flat, whom we were told was slim and probably dark. The clothes were alike in both cases.

"This was the real cleverness of the plot, for the two involved had definitely tried to merge their identities and so confuse the trail. They stressed superficial similarities and so led to attempts at identification which closer investigation was bound to discredit.

"They succeeded pretty well, as you know. Of the people who saw Fordham, neither Nurse Edwards nor Miss Godfrey had ever seen him before the evening of the 20th. Afterwards Miss Godfrey met him at her aunt's house, but not only was he differently dressed, and naturally she saw him then without his hat on, in addition, he took the precaution of altering his appearance a little, faked a cut on his face and put on plaster, drawing up his lip a little—a small thing which alters a person a good deal. Nurse Edwards he could avoid, and he did. He took care she should never see him again, sending his wife to inquire after her, and all that. So I got no recognition from either of them.

"Then the third person who had seen the murderer—Henry Godfrey. His evidence threw me off the track at first, as it was meant to. He knew Mr. Fordham quite well; he did not identify him, and in fact gave a slightly different description from the one his sister gave.

"Now, when that day, after seeing you, doctor, and Mrs. Fordham, I was thinking this all out afresh, I got a flash of light on the whole picture. When Mrs. Fordham at last told of her visit to her uncle, *she* gave me the reason for the whole crime taking place later than it had been intended. *You* gave me the idea that there had been a watcher in the street who wasn't necessarily the man in the flat. *If* Fordham were the man in the flat, then quite deliberately Godfrey had not admitted having recognized him, and was, in consequence, an accomplice."

Chapter XVI

THE COMPLETE CASE

No more riddle now, evolved at last.

The Pope, R. BROWNING.

I saw then the second point. Was Godfrey the watcher in the street?
I began to consider what I knew about him, and how far this might
be a correct hypothesis. He was, I was sure, for some reason afraid
of me. I knew he was a dealer in precious stones, and it's common
knowledge that profession is doing very badly indeed, owing to the
slump. Godfrey answered the description of the watcher which you
two had given me. One tiny little bit of information dropped into place
there, like the missing piece of a jig-saw puzzle. Godfrey had been late
for his tea-party; he'd been expected at 4.30, but hadn't arrived till just
before five. His appearance had immediately preceded the murder.
Had he been Mr. Hetherington's visitor, could he have gone across
the road, given some signal that the coast was clear, and gone in to
his tea-party and his alibi? At first this did not seem possible, for the
time given by Henry for his arrival, and that time was corroborated
by the rest of the family, who went by Mrs. Dutton's clock, did not
allow of sufficient margin. Their time fixed Henry's entry at between
ten or five minutes before five. Mr. Hetherington's visitor called, and
left his front door less than five minutes before the hour. It seemed he
could not have been the watcher, for, according to this, the watcher
was up at Mr. Hetherington's door at the moment when Henry was
safely in his aunt's flat.

"Henry knew the importance of the time, and he even knew his aunt's clock was slow. He had rung up early that morning to fix the hour for the tea-party, and had inquired of Mrs. Dutton, who spoke to him on the telephone, what time it was by her clock, making the pretext that his own watch had stopped and he was wanting to catch his train. He utilized this difference in the times to strengthen his own alibi, making his entry to Mrs. Dutton's sitting-room appear to have been made *before* five.

"In reality he had left Mr. Hetherington just before the hour, dashed down to the hotel call box, put through his call, and come back a few minutes *after* five. George, summoned by him, went up to the flat, and the fall came at ten past five. When ultimately I discovered that clock was slow, I was sure of my ground."

He glanced at his auditors, who were listening intently.

"But, Inspector," said Ainslie, "what reason had Godfrey for his actions? How came he to be involved in such a ghastly business? How did you trace his complicity?"

"At first I'd only speculation," replied Woods, "then gradually I got more facts. Of course, you must bear in mind that Godfrey never contemplated murder. The original plan must have been for robbery. Godfrey would stand for that, and I doubt if Fordham ever let fall any hint of anything worse.

"Godfrey and Fordham had known each other for some time. How Fordham originally persuaded Godfrey to help him, we'll never quite know. It may have been something to do with Mrs. Fordham. Godfrey had been in love with her before either of them married, and he'd proposed and been refused. He'd gone on being friends with her and her husband, and he may have wanted to make her life easier. You'll have noticed for yourselves, perhaps, that though he must, of course, have watched her leave Simon Ewing's flat that night and recognized who she was, he never breathed a word. He must have wanted to save her from being involved in the affair. She was the last person to have seen Mr. Ewing alive, and that made things awkward for her.

"Be that as it may, whatever induced him to do so, he did try to help the Fordhams. A couple of years ago, when he was prosperous and they weren't, he'd put his name to a bill for Fordham. When that couldn't be met this winter, owing to Fordham's more desperate position, it happened that Godfrey's own financial position had changed very much for the worse. He couldn't meet the call, and a crash meant exposure of his difficulties and probably ruin. He was up against a wall, and no doubt Fordham knew how to work on this. No one liked Simon Ewing, and everyone felt he ought to have done more to help his only relations.

"In any case, we know now that these two planned the robbery with the idea that once Fordham had secured the jewels, Godfrey would know how to dispose of them. It may seem extraordinary to you that men of good position should plan anything of the sort, but I assure you that if people are really desperate there's hardly anything they won't bring themselves to do in the end. At first, of course, it's just a sort of wish that crosses their minds—'If I only had some of that stuff lying idle up there! It does no good to anyone and it would save me'—then it becomes a definite desire developing into a determination, and the real nature and consequences of the action are blurred and almost lost sight of.

"Now once they'd decided on seeking this way out of their difficulties, they had to arrange everything most carefully. They arranged to dress alike as far as practicable, in the first place. Then they fixed the day of the tea-party and the attack on Nurse Edwards, which was carried out by Godfrey, who lay in wait for her round the corner, knowing her usual time for her outing. George had an alibi for that early period, and for what they thought would be the time when the watching had to be done in the street. Godfrey, of course, had his alibi for the actual time of the robbery. He would be at the party in Mrs. Dutton's flat. By getting up the tea-party, he made it easy for him to be in the street beforehand, in case, by ill luck, anyone recognized him, and he also made sure of one other important thing, namely that the Dutton household would be occupied in their own rooms, and not be coming in and out of their flat at the all-important time."

"How did they arrange for Fordham to know when the coast was clear?" put in Hetherington.

"He'd been at intervals during the past month to that big billiard saloon in the High Street, always at about 4 o'clock or earlier. Once or twice he'd been rung up there, under the name of Clutton. We've traced these calls and found that they were made from Godfrey's office. This got the people there accustomed to fetching him to the telephone. On the night in question, as soon as Godfrey knew the coast was clear, he dashed down the street to the call box that was put in just by the hotel, not a minute away. He was ringing up from there when Dr. Ainslie went home. It didn't take Fordham more than two minutes to come round. Godfrey must have waited in the box, seen him pass, and then followed up Clevedon Street and gone in to Mrs. Dutton."

"Yes," said Ainslie, "I suppose that time-table was bound to work out. But, Inspector, however much you guessed of all this, you hadn't any clear proof."

"No, but I had other lines to work on. The time factor gave me the idea as to the conception of the crime. Then I had one other definite fact to take into account. These rings were missing. I'd not much hope the man would be fool enough to try and dispose of them in the ordinary way through shops and pawnbrokers. He might later on, through Godfrey, but it wasn't greatly to be expected. Still, I thought I'd probably get at the truth through the Godfrey end. I suspected those big diamonds would pass into his hands. I was really on their track when I went back to Clevedon St. that afternoon. I wanted to go and have another look upstairs. I thought Fordham might, as an alternative, have tried at the last moment to hide those rings up there, where they'd be found when the furniture was moved out. It would be thought the murderer had put them there, and never had the time or opportunity to go back for them before he was disturbed by Godfrey and Nurse Edwards's entry. That would remove the risk he ran as long as he had them in his possession, and at the same time, as heir, he would inherit them if they were found.

"That was what I'm sure, in fact, he meant to do. The marks on the end of the cabinet were not there when I first went up. I looked most carefully all round the room, as I felt it would be my last visit. I found no trace of the rings, and no marks of any sort anywhere. The marks *were* there, and obviously fresh, when we found Mrs. Fordham's body. She hadn't made them; there was no tool on her, and nothing left in the room which might have been used. I knew too, and the medical evidence confirmed it, that she hadn't been holding those rings in her hand during life, they'd been put there after death.

"I guessed she must have gone up there, and surprised her husband in the act of trying to conceal those rings. That splinter in the cabinet showed where he had been trying to push them behind there, on the top of the wainscot edge. He'd tried first to undo a cabinet so as to conceal the rings inside, I imagine, but failed, as he daren't tamper with the lock; when he got the seal loosened he saw it was too risky a job, so he tried a simpler place. He probably put them down beside him while he began to poke with his knife at the place where the cabinet met the wainscot. When she came in, she'd have a direct view of the hearth, and the cabinet, and of him. She would see what he was up to, and I expect saw the rings at once.

"Of course that gave him away completely. Everyone knew by then that whoever had got those rings had murdered Mr. Ewing.

I expect his face and his attitude made his guilt perfectly obvious to her. I'm afraid she showed him what she realized, and he, without any hesitation, silenced *her.* "

For a moment the inspector stopped. Neither of his companions spoke. They knew that the scene he reconstructed in such quiet, controlled tones had taken place only a few yards from where they sat. They visualized the young wife's entry into the flat she thought empty—the sight of her husband crouching down on the hearth by the cabinet, the rings, perhaps, glittering beside him—his glance up as the door opened, the pause while each took in the other's attitude and knowledge, and then the swift advance upon the woman, her short struggle, and its end.

Dr. Ainslie gave a deep sigh. "Poor thing. She hadn't a chance, she was so slight and delicate. It must have been soon over."

Woods nodded, rather grimly. "It was. I know that. Mr. Hetherington here looked out of his window and saw her go in just before half-past three. Fordham was in that pub round the corner, having a stiff drink, by a quarter to four."

For a moment he left that brief statement to sink in. Then, with a lightening of his tone, went on:

"I saw at once the implications of this second crime. The details really revealed a great deal.

"Mrs. Fordham had been thrown on the sofa, and suffocated there. That, to me, implied that the murderer wished to have no repetition of the noise made by Mr. Ewing's fall. That, in turn, showed he knew all the details of the first crime, and he knew there were people below who'd come up this time if they heard any noise at all.

"I soon discovered that Mrs. Fordham had been expected at the flat at 4 o'clock. Miss Godfrey knew all about that. I traced the proposed visit to the dentist, and heard she'd cancelled it at 3.15, and saw at once that she had come unexpectedly early, had gone straight upstairs, and, arriving at about 3.30 instead of at 4, interrupted someone who was trying to hide those rings. Who had been expecting her to arrive at 4 o'clock? Her husband and Miss Godfrey.

"Miss Godfrey wasn't either the murderer or the watcher in Mr. Ewing's case, so I knew at once this second crime was Fordham's. After the rings were tested, his fingerprints were found on one of them, on the inside of the jade. He'd closed her hand over the outside, and I suppose was too flustered to think he might have left a print of his own on the inside.

"We had a complete case against him now. I could prove he'd handled those rings, had indeed pushed them into his wife's hand. I'd dug out his fraud on his employer. I could piece together my facts, and I'd enough to hang him. I still hadn't quite enough though, I feared, to get Godfrey.

"I'd nothing very definite against him. Just his money difficulties, his connexion with Fordham, and I hoped, his resemblance to the watcher. It wasn't quite enough.

"I believed, if we took Fordham in front of Godfrey, he might give himself away, or, knowing himself done for, Fordham might accuse him.

"I felt it was the best plan I could hit on, so I arranged it, as you know. I got Fordham there; I got him to call on you, Mr. Hetherington, so that you should see him ringing at your door much as you'd seen the watcher. You came across and assured me he wasn't the man you'd seen before. I'd had a man outside to tell me when Godfrey turned the corner of the street. As soon as I got his signal—you remember the knock that came at the door—I went in to make the arrest of Fordham. Godfrey, who had been brought to the house by a telephone message we sent, came in the mistaken belief that he must see Fordham at once, as something had gone wrong, arrived to find the police in the very act of securing his accomplice by force. He realized what it all meant, knew his chances of Fordham keeping him out of it were very slight, and preferred to end it in his own way."

After a brief silence, in which all three reflected on the slow development of the double crime, Woods went on:

"So you see how I could, after the second crime, reconstruct the stages in the whole affair. First the planning of the robbery, then the mischances which turned it to murder, then the catastrophe of the second death. Godfrey, of course, must have been utterly appalled at the dreadful way it all turned out.

"I think we can tell now, pretty well, what was done. First they considered how to get the money needed to save them both, and they evolved the idea of stealing the jewellery.

"Their plan was simple and bold. Fordham would go up, in the absence of Nurse, and ring. He would probably persist, call out perhaps, until his uncle let him in. He'd make, possibly, a last effort to get a loan or gift from the old man, and he'd fail. Then he'd pretend to leave. He could be sure his uncle wouldn't get up and let him out. He might slam the front door, as an act in keeping with the scene. He wouldn't go out, however; he'd slip upstairs to the empty room, where he knew the box was kept. If that box had been in its usual place, all might have been different. As you know, Mr. Ewing had moved the box that very afternoon, taking advantage of his niece visiting him in the nurse's absence. Fordham found the box gone; he was desperate; he was always of a violent disposition. He *may* have meant, when he went back to the drawing room, to take it by force, and trust to his uncle not denouncing him, but I expect he never even stopped to think. He meant to have that stuff, and when he found it moved, he went to get it from his uncle. He struck the old man down just before the nurse arrived back. The nurse came ringing at the door—he daren't risk her coming in, going straight to that room, and finding him there. He killed the old man, and dashed up to the empty room, as you know, then bluffed his way out and away.

"Godfrey probably never envisaged what had happened. He must have hoped, when he saw Fordham come from the bedroom, that he'd simply got to cover the tracks of a burglary. What he felt later, we can only tell from what he did—decided his position was unendurable, and took his own life."

"How had Fordham got into the flat the second time?" inquired Hetherington, who had been listening intently.

"He'd got duplicate keys. He'd been given one set by the police, and that set he handed to his wife. He'd had another set made—we haven't traced where, but we found them after the arrest in one of his drawers. If we'd challenged his possession earlier, he could always have said he'd found them in his uncle's flat, and we couldn't have proved anything against that."

"If he *had* got away safely with the jewellery, wouldn't his uncle have suspected him?"

"Not necessarily. That was where Godfrey came in. As a dealer he'd have unique opportunities of getting rid of the stones and breaking up the ornaments. I don't think it would ever have been traced. Mr. Ewing would probably not have discovered the theft for weeks or months, for he practically never looked at the contents of the box. By that time he would almost certainly have changed his nurse, once at least, if not more often. He never kept one very long. Suspicion would have fallen on the nurse. He would never have suspected George hadn't left the flat that evening."

"H'm, well, that sounds plausible certainly," said Ainslie. "And I suppose, anyway, a desperate man will take desperate risks."

"Yes," answered Woods. "And you know only one thing put their plans wrong. If Mrs. Fordham had never gone in to visit her uncle, it would all have been over and done with an hour earlier. The nurse would have come back to an empty flat. Godfrey wouldn't have had to go up with her, Fordham would have found the box, for the old man couldn't fetch it down himself, and so it all would have gone right instead of wrong."

"Ah, yes!" said Hetherington, "you're right, I imagine. Time turned against them. It's usually the test of everything in this world."